W9-BST-345
این کتاب را برای شما خریدم
امیدوارم که دوست داشته باشی

مامان هما

Nancy Drew

* CLUE BOOK *

4 books in 1!

Nancy Drew
CLUE BOOK

4 books in 1!

Pool Party Puzzler

Last Lemonade Standing

A Star Witness

Big Top Flop

BY CAROLYN KEENE * ILLUSTRATED BY PETER FRANCIS

Aladdin

NEW YORK LONDON TORONTO SYDNEY NEW DELHI

This book is a work of fiction. Any references to historical events, real people, or real places are used fictitiously. Other names, characters, places, and events are products of the author's imagination, and any resemblance to actual events or places or persons, living or dead, is entirely coincidental.

ALADDIN
An imprint of Simon & Schuster Children's Publishing Division
1230 Avenue of the Americas, New York, NY 10020
This Aladdin hardcover edition March 2019

For information about special discounts for bulk purchases, please contact Simon & Schuster Special Sales at 1-866-506-1949 or business@simonandschuster.com.
The Simon & Schuster Speakers Bureau can bring authors to your live event.
For more information or to book an event contact the Simon & Schuster Speakers Bureau at 1-866-248-3049 or visit our website at www.simonspeakers.com.
Books designed by Karina Granda
The illustrations for this book were rendered digitally.
The text of this book was set in Adobe Garamond Pro.
Manufactured in the United States of America 1219 FFG
2 4 6 8 10 9 7 5 3
Library of Congress Control Number 2019930236
ISBN 978-1-5344-5353-1 (hc)
ISBN 978-1-4814-2938-2 (*Pool Party Puzzler* eBook)
ISBN 978-1-4814-3749-3 (*Last Lemonade Standing* eBook)
ISBN 978-1-4814-3751-6 (*A Star Witness* eBook)
ISBN 978-1-4814-3753-0 (*Big Top Flop* eBook)
These titles were previously published individually.

* CONTENTS *

Pool Party Puzzler

THRONE . . . AND GROANS

"I've heard of sweet sixteen parties before," George Fayne said, "but whoever heard of a sweet *half*-sixteen?"

Nancy Drew looked up from the goody bag she was filling for Deirdre Shannon's sweet half-sixteen party.

"Eight is half of sixteen," Nancy explained. "So since Deirdre is turning eight, she asked her parents for a sweet half-sixteen party!"

"And whatever Deirdre wants," Bess Marvin

said, dropping a fancy iced cookie into a bag, "Deirdre gets!"

It was summer vacation and the theme of Deirdre's party was Beach Party Blast. Nancy, Bess, and George had come extra early to help George's mom cater the party. Louise Fayne had catered lots of kids' birthday parties, but nothing as fancy as this!

"We're eight years old and half-sixteen, too," Nancy pointed out. "And we have something just as awesome as a party like this."

"What?" Bess asked.

"Our own detective club called the Clue Crew!" Nancy answered with a smile.

Nancy, Bess, and George high-fived. The three best friends loved solving mysteries more than anything. They even had their own detective headquarters in Nancy's room!

"And my dad just gave me this brand-new notebook," Nancy said, pulling a notebook with a shiny red cover from her bag. "He told me it would be a good place to write down suspects and clues for our cases. I'm going to call it the Clue Book!"

Nancy's father wasn't a detective, but he was a lawyer. To Nancy that was the next best thing.

"But we already write down all of our suspects on your computer, Nancy," George pointed out. George loved electronic gadgets more than anything!

"That's true." Nancy nodded. "But we can take the Clue Book with us wherever we go. It will make us even *better* detectives!"

"Okay, if we're such great detectives," George said, "then why are we all dressed up so goofy?"

"Deirdre asked everyone to wear sea costumes over our swimsuits," Nancy reminded her. "I'm a sea horse, Bess is a sea fairy, and you're a—"

"Jellyfish!" George groaned. The ribbon tentacles streaming from her hat wiggled over her face. "Don't remind me."

Nancy brushed aside her reddish-blond bangs to look around for Deirdre. She was probably getting ready for her grand entrance. Mrs. Fayne said it would be at one o'clock sharp—after the guests arrived.

"Great job, girls," Mrs. Fayne said after all the goody bags had been stuffed and placed on a table. "Why don't you explore the yard before the others get here?"

Nancy smiled as she looked around the Shannons' backyard. It looked more like a beach than a yard. There was real white sand and beach umbrellas around the pool. On each party table was a sand castle centerpiece surrounded by shells and starfish. Inflated palm trees dotted the lawn. So did some of Deirdre's birthday presents—like a shiny lavender electric scooter with a matching helmet!

"This party is going to be amazing," George said. "I'll bet every kid in River Heights is invited."

"Every kid but Shelby Metcalf," Nancy said. "Deirdre is still mad at Shelby for not trading lunches with her at school one day."

"What kind of lunches?" Bess asked.

"Shelby had peanut butter and jelly," Nancy explained. "Deirdre had a soggy spinach salad."

George suddenly stopped walking. "Hey, check it out!" she said, pointing to something in the distance.

Nancy and Bess looked to see where George was pointing. A woman wearing a sun hat was busily snipping hedges behind the pool. The three hedges were shaped like sea creatures!

"Let's get a closer look!" Nancy said excitedly.

The girls hurried over to the woman. She was in the middle of trimming the claw on a hedge shaped like a crab.

"Hello," Bess said. "Are you a gardener?"

"I'm what they call a garden designer," the woman replied with a cheery smile. "My name is Taffy, and I create topiaries." She pointed at one of the leafy hedges.

"To-pi-ar-ies," Nancy repeated.

"Topiaries by Taffy," Taffy said proudly. "That's the name of my company!"

"Did Deirdre see these topiaries yet?" George asked.

"If she did," Bess said, "I'd bet she loved them!"

But Taffy shook her head and heaved a sigh.

"Deirdre wasn't very happy with my topiaries," Taffy said. "She wanted one of them to look like her!"

"You mean she wanted a grassy statue of herself?" George asked.

Taffy nodded and said, "Deirdre said she was Queen of the Sea and her party had to be *perfect*."

"That sounds like Deirdre, all right," Bess said.

"Oh well," Taffy said. She gave her topiary

one final snip. "I guess I'll have to surprise Queen Deirdre later."

Nancy wondered what the surprise would be. Before she got a chance to ask, Bess shook Nancy's arm.

"The other guests are here!" Bess announced.

Nancy turned to see other kids dressed like sea creatures in the Shannons' backyard. The most awesome party of the year was about to begin!

After saying a quick good-bye to Taffy, the girls ran to join the others. Many were dancing. Some were sipping smoothies.

Nancy recognized Kendra Jackson, Marcy Rubin, and Henderson Murphy from school. But there was one kid no one knew.

"Who's that?" George asked. She nodded toward a kid wearing a green sea monster costume. A mask and headdress totally covered his or her face. Both hands were stuffed inside gloves with long webbed fingers!

"I know how we can find out," Nancy said

with a smile. "Let's go over and say hi."

The girls walked over to the sea monster kid.

"Hi, there. That's a neat costume," Bess said kindly. "But aren't you hot in it?"

The kid shook his or her head, then walked away without a word.

"We still don't know who she is," Bess said.

"How do you know she's a *she*?" Nancy asked.

"Her feet weren't covered," Bess said. "Did you see her purple sandals and pink toenail polish? Totally girlie-girl."

"Like you, Bess!" George teased. "Only *you* would notice purple sandals and pink toenail polish!"

Nancy giggled. Bess and George were cousins but totally different. Bess had blond hair and blue eyes, and she loved clothes more than anything. George had dark eyes and curly hair. She was fine with new clothes as long as they had enough pockets for her electronic gadgets!

"I have an idea," Nancy suggested. "Let's get some smoothies—before the tropical ones are gone."

"Last one there is a rotten coconut!" George declared.

They were about to run to the party's special smoothie stand when a big voice boomed through a DJ's speakers. "Attention, kids! Let's give it up for everybody's favorite sweet half-sixteen birthday girl, Queen Deirdre of the Sea!"

"It's Deirdre's grand entrance!" Nancy said excitedly. She glanced at her watch. It was one o'clock. "And right on schedule!"

The kids gathered on the patio to watch. A trumpet blared as four teenagers wearing huge fish headdresses marched around the side of the house. In each of their hands was a pole. Resting atop the four poles was a giant half-shell throne!

Nancy couldn't believe her eyes. Waving down from the elaborate shell was Deirdre. The birthday girl was dressed in a glitzy mermaid costume and shell-covered crown!

"Awesome!" Nancy exclaimed.

The teens made a sudden sharp turn and the

throne tipped. Deirdre screamed as it swayed back and forth!

"Oh, noooo!" Nancy shrieked as she covered her eyes. "Queen Deirdre is going to fall!"

Chapter 2

NOT COOL IN THE POOL

"Steady, you guys!" one of the teens shouted. "Bring it down easy . . . nice and easy."

Nancy peeked out from between her fingers. Both the shell throne and Deirdre were slowly being lowered onto the ground.

The party guests sighed with relief. But Deirdre hopped off the throne hopping mad!

"You should have been more careful. After all, you were carrying a queen's throne!" Deirdre scolded. "Not some tray at Crabby Carl's!"

Deirdre gave the teens one last glare and ran off to join her friends. The four teens stood to the side, frowns on their faces.

"I thought those fish hats looked familiar," Bess said. "Those teenagers are waiters at Crabby Carl's Seafood Restaurant!"

"The waiters look pretty crabby right now," George whispered. "After being yelled at by Queen Deirdre."

"I feel bad for the fish teens," Nancy said. "Let's tell them they did a great job!"

Nancy, Bess, and George walked toward the teenagers. As they got nearer they heard them talking in lowered voices.

"Deirdre Shannon has been bossing us around since we started practicing," a girl was saying.

"She's a queen, all right," another girl said. "The queen of mean!"

"Forget about it," one boy said. He flashed a sly smile. "Because it's time to carry out our secret plan."

The teens' fish headdresses wiggled as they

bumped fists. They then turned and walked around to the side of the house.

"Secret plan?" Nancy asked. "What secret plan?"

"It wouldn't be a secret if we knew!" George shrugged.

Nancy wanted to know. She was about to suggest following the teens when—

"Attention, kids!" Mrs. Shannon shouted into a bullhorn. "Please follow Queen Deirdre into the house so you can hang up your costumes."

"Then everybody into the pool!" Deirdre cried, her hands waving in the air.

The kids cheered. Nancy forgot about the teens and their secret plan as she, Bess, and George followed Deirdre and the others.

As they walked around the swimming pool, Nancy glanced into the water. It was crystal clear all the way down to the bottom. Perfect for swimming!

"Hey, you guys," George said, interrupting Nancy's thoughts. "There's the sea monster."

Nancy turned to see the kid in the sea monster costume. Instead of following the others, the monster lagged behind.

"Aren't you coming too?" Nancy called.

The sea monster shook her head, which was still totally covered.

"Oh well," Nancy said as she and her friends continued walking. "Maybe she didn't bring her swimsuit."

"I brought three suits," Bess said with a smile. "The one under my costume plus two other options."

"Give me a break!" George groaned.

Once inside the house, the kids hung up their costumes. Nancy carefully put the Clue Book into her bag, and hung up her bag beside her costume. George couldn't wait to get out of her jellyfish suit!

"Hurry up, hurry up!" Deirdre cried. She was now wearing a bright blue swimsuit with her Queen of the Sea crown. "My parents have *another* big surprise for me outside."

"Bigger than the electric scooter?" Henderson asked.

"I hope so!" Deirdre said. She gave a little jump and squealed, "You guys—is my super sweet half-sixteen party perfect or what?"

When all the costumes were hung on racks, Deirdre rushed everyone to the back door. Deirdre was the first outside for her latest surprise. Nancy could see Deirdre's jaw drop as she stared straight ahead.

Nancy followed Deirdre's gaze. What she saw was a beautiful mermaid seated on a gold throne decorated with pink and silver seashells!

"Happy birthday, Deirdre!" the mermaid called as she waved. "It's so good to 'sea' you. That's s-e-a, as in the ocean. Hee-hee!"

Deirdre turned to her parents. "You got me a mermaid?" she asked.

"Not just *any* mermaid, honey," Mr. Shannon said. "It's Marissa—Queen of the Mermaids!"

"I've come to swim for you all today!" Mermaid Marissa exclaimed, still waving her hand.

"Okay, kids," Mrs. Shannon called to the guests. "Who wants to meet Queen Marissa?"

"Me, me, me!" everyone shouted.

Nancy, Bess, and George raced straight to Queen Marissa's throne with the others. Those with cameras or phones took pictures of the glittering mermaid.

"How about a picture with the birthday girl?" Mr. Shannon asked, holding up a camera. He looked around. "Where did Deirdre disappear to, anyway?"

"Over here!" Deirdre shouted.

Nancy turned to see Deirdre squeezing through the crowd. When she reached the mermaid's throne she flashed a smile for the camera.

"And now," Queen Marissa said with a shake of her fin, "it's time for my spectacular deep-sea swim show!"

The DJ played soft music as bubbles drifted from machines. Excited whispers also filled the air as Queen Marissa hobbled across the diving board. When she reached the edge, she raised both hands gracefully above her head.

"She's going to dive!" Nancy said.

"I've never seen a mermaid swim before," Bess said.

"This is going to be good," George declared.

Marissa gave a little hop. But just as she was about to jump, she froze to a stop.

"Look!" Marissa screamed as she pointed down at the water. "At the bottom of the pool. Th-th-there's a snake!"

SNAKY SHOCKER

Everyone began talking at once.

"In the pool?"

"A real live snake?"

"No way!"

Mr. and Mrs. Shannon kept the kids away from the pool, but the green and yellow snake coiled at the bottom wasn't hard to see.

"Ew!" Bess shrieked.

"You don't see that every day!" George said.

That's for sure, Nancy thought. She knew she hadn't seen a snake in the pool when she had looked in it earlier!

Mr. Shannon rushed to help Queen Marissa off the diving board. He tried to apologize, but she wouldn't hear it.

"I'm out of here!" Marissa declared. "No more kiddie parties for me—ever!"

Nancy couldn't take her eyes off of the snake. It wasn't moving. And it looked like something was hanging from its tail!

"Mr. and Mrs. Shannon?" Nancy called. "I think that snake has a tag on its tail."

"A tag?" Mr. Shannon said.

Using a skimmer, one of the caterers helped fish the snake out of the pool. The snake did have a tag on its tail—a price tag!

"Guess what, boys and girls?" Mr. Shannon chuckled with relief. "This snake is a fake!"

"It sure is!" Mrs. Shannon said, reading the tag. "It's from Yuks Joke Shop on Main Street!"

"Some joke!" Deirdre snapped. She turned

to glare at her party guests. "Okay, which one of you jokers threw that fake snake into the pool?"

The kids stared blankly at Deirdre, not saying a word. Some mumbled "Not me" or "Nuh-uh."

Mrs. Shannon put a gentle hand on Deirdre's shoulder.

"Deirdre, dear," she said. "Why don't we forget about that silly snake and continue with the pool party?"

"Well . . . ," Deirdre muttered. "Okay."

"You heard the queen!" Mr. Shannon boomed with a smile. "Everybody into the pool!"

Deirdre was smiling again as the kids grabbed swim rafts and floatation noodles. But as the others hopped into the pool, Nancy, Bess, and George stood to the side, talking softly.

"I think Deirdre was right," Nancy admitted. "Someone here must have thrown that snake into the pool."

"Maybe it wasn't just a dumb joke either,"

George said. "Maybe somebody wanted to ruin Deirdre's party."

"Who would want to ruin an awesome party like this one?" Bess asked.

"I don't know," Nancy said. "But I think the Clue Crew should find out."

Bess gave a little hop as she clapped her hands. Parties were fun, but so were solving mysteries—especially for the Clue Crew!

"Okay," George said. "Let's tell Deirdre we're on the case."

"I'm sure she'll be happy we want to help!" Bess said.

But when Nancy, Bess, and George offered to find the snake slinger, Deirdre shook her head.

"This is a pool party!" Deirdre replied firmly. "Not some mystery party!"

Nancy, Bess, and George stared openmouthed at Deirdre as she huffed away. Still wearing her crown, she jumped into the pool with a big splash.

"I guess she doesn't want us to solve this mystery." Bess sighed.

"Deirdre may not want to solve this mystery," Nancy said. "But I do."

"So do I," George said. She cracked a little smile. "If you ask me, something *fishy* is going on around here."

"George, puh-leeze!" Bess groaned.

The girls didn't want to leave the party for their detective headquarters. Instead they discussed the case floating on a lobster raft in the pool.

"I'm sure the snake was thrown in right before Queen Marissa's show," Nancy said.

"Probably while we were all in the house."

"How do you know?" George asked.

"I peeked in the pool right before we went inside," Nancy explained. "The water looked great. There were no snakes!"

The lobster raft drifted past other kids splashing in the pool. Everybody looked so happy—not angry or mean!

"I still don't get it," Bess said. "Who would want to ruin such a great party?"

"Maybe somebody who was mad at Deirdre," Nancy said with a shrug.

"Everybody is mad at Deirdre at some point," George said. "She's always yelling at people."

Yelling? Nancy's eyes lit up at the word.

"What about the waiters from Crabby Carl's?" Nancy suggested. "They were mad at Deirdre for yelling at them."

"And they said something about a secret plan," Bess added. "Maybe their plan was that icky snake."

"The waiters are our first suspects," George

declared. "But who else would want to ruin Deirdre's party?"

"It could have been any of these kids," Bess said, looking out at the swimmers. "But if we were all in the house at the time of the crime—"

"But we weren't all in the house!" Nancy cut in. "Remember the sea monster? She didn't want to come inside!"

"We never saw her again after that either," George pointed out.

"The sea monster is our next suspect," Bess declared. "Whoever she is."

"I want to make a list of our suspects like we always do," George said.

"Let's get the Clue Book!" Nancy said.

"Come on. I left it in the house."

The girls left the lobster raft floating in the pool as they stepped out. On the way they passed by Taffy's topiaries. Nancy's favorite was the angelfish. But just as she went to get a closer look . . .

"Nancy!" Bess cried. "Watch out!"

SOMETHING FISHY

"What?" Nancy asked. She looked down and gasped. Curled up in the grass just inches away from her feet was another snake!

"Omigosh! Omigosh!" Bess cried.

"Calm down," George said. "That one is fake too!"

George pointed to the Yuks price tag on the snake's tail. It was also the same color as the snake in the pool—green and yellow!

"There's one more!" Nancy exclaimed, pointing

to another fake snake by the second topiary. The girls checked out the third one but didn't find any fake snake.

"Do you think Taffy planted all these snakes?" Nancy asked. "The one in the pool, too?"

"Why would Taffy want to spoil Deirdre's party?" Bess asked.

"Taffy told us that Deirdre didn't like her topiaries," Nancy said. "Then Taffy said she had a surprise for Deirdre."

"Maybe Taffy's surprise was the fake snake in the pool!" George said. "I guess Taffy is our next suspect."

"Do you still want to write down the list of suspects in the Clue Book, Nancy?" Bess asked.

"I'd rather go back to the party," Nancy admitted. "Even detectives need a break once in a while."

"Especially after finding those snakes!" Bess shuddered.

The rest of the party was awesome. The girls didn't find any more fake snakes. Deirdre seemed happy too as she thanked her guests for coming to her "perfect" super sweet half-sixteen party.

After the party Nancy, Bess, and George helped Mrs. Fayne and the caterers pack up all the leftover food and supplies. They were happy to snack on some extra cookies and mini quiche while Nancy listed all their suspects in the Clue Book. At the top of the list she wrote:

1. Crabby Carl's waiters

Then she wrote:

2. Taffy of Taffy's Topiaries
3. Sea monster

"I'd like to stop off at Crabby Carl's," Mrs. Fayne said as she drove the girls home in her catering van. "Those waiters worked so hard that I think they deserve some cupcakes."

Nancy, Bess, and George traded looks. The waiters at Crabby Carl's were suspects!

"Um, we can drop off the cupcakes, Mrs. Fayne!"

Nancy blurted. "We want to visit Crabby Carl's anyway."

"Why?" Mrs. Fayne asked, sounding surprised.

"Er, to visit Crusty the lobster," George said quickly. "You know, the lobster that's been in their tank for years and years."

"We love Crusty!" Bess added.

"Okay, okay." Mrs. Fayne chuckled. "Crabby Carl's is within five blocks of our house."

"Thanks, Mrs. Fayne!" Nancy exclaimed.

Nancy, Bess, and George had the same rule: They could walk anywhere without an adult as long as it was within five blocks of home and as long as they were together.

"Be careful with those cupcakes," Mrs. Fayne warned as she dropped off the girls at Crabby Carl's. "And say hi to Crusty for me!"

"We will, Mom!" George called as she carried the big box of cupcakes.

Nancy, Bess, and George walked through a pair of swinging doors into the restaurant. Tables were filled with people eating fish, hush puppies, and Nancy's favorite popcorn shrimp!

"Can I help you?" someone with a gruff voice asked.

Nancy, Bess, and George turned to see Crabby Carl, the owner of the restaurant. He got his nickname because he hardly ever smiled, but his food was great!

"What are those? Cupcakes?" Carl asked, staring through the box's cellophane cover. "We serve our own desserts here."

"I know," George said. "My mom is a caterer."

"And she wants the waiters who worked at Deirdre Shannon's party to have these cupcakes," Nancy added.

"Cupcakes for the waiters?" Carl growled. "What about for me? I own the place!"

"If they're nice, they'll share!" Bess said.

"Okay," Carl said. He nodded to the back of the

restaurant and said, "You can bring the cupcakes to the waiters' break room. The ones who worked at the party are busy serving customers now, but they should be taking their break any minute now."

"Thank you, Mr. Crabby," Nancy said.

The girls were about to head to the back when they noticed something strange. For the first time the lobster tank in the restaurant was empty.

"What happened to Crusty?" George asked.

"I don't know." Crabby Carl sighed sadly. "One minute Crusty was in the tank; the next minute he was gone!"

As the girls headed to the back, Bess whispered, "You don't think someone ate Crusty, do you?"

"Who would want to eat Crusty?" George demanded. "He's like a celebrity here!"

The waiters' break room was next to the kitchen. George opened the door, and the girls stepped inside. They looked around and saw a lumpy brown sofa, table, TV, fridge, and a wooden room divider that looked like a screen.

"The waiters aren't here yet," Nancy said as George placed the cupcake box on the table. "Let's look for clues!"

"What kind of clues?" Bess asked.

"Start searching for fake snakes," George suggested. "Maybe there's a box of them around here somewhere."

Nancy, Bess, and George searched the room until they heard voices outside the door.

"The waiters are coming!" George whispered. "Let's hide so we can listen to what they say."

The three friends darted behind the screen.

They peeked out through the screen's wooden slats. Four waiters were stepping into the room wearing fish headdresses.

"That's them," George hissed. "The same waiters from the party!"

"I hope they don't find us snooping," Bess whispered.

The girls were as quiet as mice as they listened. Nancy couldn't resist taking out the Clue Book. She wanted to make sure to write down anything important that the waiters said.

"Mission accomplished, you guys," a boy said. "And nobody had a clue it was us!"

Nancy shot her friends a sideways glance. Was their mission putting the snake into Deirdre's pool?

"Now it's on to Plan B!" the boy went on.

"Plan B?" Nancy whispered. "What's Plan B?"

The girls peered through the slats again. This time they all gasped. The waiters were walking toward them! One of the waiters carried a big white container, which she placed on the ground just a few inches from Nancy.

Another waiter suddenly stopped. She pointed to the table and said, "Cupcakes! Let's have some before we get started on our plan."

As the waiters helped themselves to the cupcakes, George tugged on Nancy's elbow.

"Look!" George whispered. She nodded toward the white container. "Maybe the fake snakes are in there!"

Nancy, Bess, and George gathered around the container. Cold air blasted out as George pulled off the lid. Inside was a pile of ice and something else. . . .

"Holy cannoli," George whispered.

"It's a giant cockroach!" Bess cried.

"That's not a cockroach!" Nancy said. She stared down at the dark red creature waving its claws. "That's *Crusty*!"

TOE*NAILED*

The girls shrieked as Crusty tried crawling out of the container. They ran out from behind the screen one by one.

When the waiters saw the girls, they froze with the cupcakes still in their hands. Nancy could see their names stitched on their aprons: NICOLE, KIERAN, TODD, and JESSICA.

"Um . . . hi." Nancy gulped.

"What are you kids doing here?" Nicole demanded.

"We brought those cupcakes you're eating," George said.

"Yummy, huh?" Bess asked.

"If you just brought cupcakes," Todd said, "why were you hiding?"

"We wanted to find out who threw the fake snake into Deirdre's pool," George said bravely. "Was it you guys?"

"There was a fake snake in Deirdre Shannon's pool?" Todd asked, sounding surprised.

"I'm sorry we missed that!" Nicole chuckled.

"You should be sorry," Bess said. "It almost ruined Deirdre's party."

"I am sorry about that," Nicole admitted. "But it wasn't us."

"We left right after Deirdre's grand entrance," Jessica said. "We didn't see any snakes in the pool."

"But we know Deirdre yelled at you," Nancy said. "We also heard you talking about some secret plan."

The four waiters began to laugh.

"What's so funny?" George demanded.

"Our secret plan is to free Crusty before his sixtieth birthday," Jessica explained.

"Free Crusty?" Nancy repeated.

"Carl doesn't know it," Jessica said in a hushed voice. "But I'm going to take Crusty on our family vacation to the sea tomorrow."

"You mean you're going to throw him back into the ocean?" Bess asked, wide-eyed.

"Sure thing," Kieran replied. "Crusty is going to love it!"

Nancy understood it now. So that's why Crusty wasn't in his tank. He was about to be freed!

Suddenly, Kieran pointed over Nancy's, Bess's, and George's shoulders and cried, "There's Crusty!"

Nancy, Bess, and George whirled around. Crusty the lobster had escaped the container and was scrambling across the floor!

"Crusty can't be out of that container for long!" Kieran exclaimed. "We've got to put him back on ice now!"

But Crusty had other plans. The lobster picked

up speed and took off. Nancy, Bess, and George watched the waiters chase Crusty through the room.

"The waiters seem nice," Nancy whispered. "But how do we know they really left after Deirdre's grand entrance?"

"I know how we can find out," George whispered. "Follow me."

The waiters were still chasing Crusty as the girls walked over to a clock on the wall.

"This is called a time clock," George explained. "The waiters stick a card inside, and it prints the time they got to work."

A rack of time cards hung next to the clock. Quickly and quietly the girls found the cards for Nicole, Kieran, Todd, and Jessica.

"Deirdre's grand entrance was at one o'clock sharp," Nancy whispered. "These cards show that the waiters got to work at one thirty."

"So they *did* go straight to work," Bess whispered.

Suddenly—

"Gotcha!" Jessica shouted as she grabbed Crusty. The waiters cheered until someone else burst into the room. It was Carl . . . and he looked crabby!

"What's that racket back here?" Carl said. His eyes flew wide open when he saw the lobster in Jessica's hands. "Cheese and crackers! Is that Crusty?"

"Um . . . ," Todd started to say.

Nicole stalled. "Well . . ."

"Time to go," Nancy murmured to Bess and George.

The girls left the break room and the restaurant. As they stepped outside, George said, "So the fish are off the hook. What next?"

"It's getting late," Nancy said. "Let's work on the case tomorrow."

"Good idea, Nancy," George said. "I'm getting hungry for dinner—even after all that party food."

"What are you eating tonight, George?" Bess asked.

"Anything but lobster!" George groaned.

"Would you like grilled veggies with your burger, Nancy?" Mr. Drew called from the grill in the backyard. He was wearing the DUDE WITH THE FOOD apron Nancy had given him for Father's Day.

"Yes, thanks, Daddy!" Nancy said. "I'd also like some help with the Clue Crew's new case, please."

"One order of mystery advice coming right up!" Mr. Drew declared.

As Nancy played on the grass with her puppy, Chocolate Chip, she explained the case of the fake snake in the pool. She had already crossed off the waiters' names from the list of suspects in the Clue Book:

1. ~~Crabby Carl's waiters~~
2. Taffy of Taffy's Topiaries
3. Sea monster

"The waiters didn't do it," Nancy said. "We already figured that out."

"Do you have any other suspects?" Mr. Drew asked.

"We have two more, Daddy," Nancy replied. "One is Taffy the garden designer. The other is that mysterious kid in the sea monster costume."

Hannah Gruen smiled as she carried a bowl of fruit salad into the backyard. Hannah was much more than the Drew's housekeeper; she was almost like a mother to Nancy. That's because Nancy's real mother died when she was only three years old.

"Do you know the sea monster kid's name?" Hannah asked.

Nancy shook her head and said, "All we know is that she likes pink toenail polish, Hannah. That's not much."

Chip's ears suddenly perked up. She wagged her tail, then raced away and around the side of the house.

"Chip, come back!" Nancy called. "You're not on a leash!"

Nancy chased Chip to the front yard. Chip was still wagging her tail and barking toward the sidewalk. Walking past the Drew's house was Shelby Metcalf.

"Hi, Shelby," Nancy said, holding on to Chip's collar. Her puppy seemed to know all of Nancy's friends!

"Oh, uh, hi, Nancy," Shelby said. She didn't look like she wanted to talk but stopped anyway. "Um . . . how was Deirdre's party?"

Nancy had totally forgotten that Shelby hadn't been invited to Deirdre's party. What could she say that wouldn't make Shelby feel bad?

"Um . . . it was okay," Nancy said with a shrug.

But as Nancy lowered her eyes she saw something that made her gasp. Shelby was wearing purple sandals. And her toenails were painted pink!

Omigosh, Nancy thought, her heart pounding. *Just like the sea monster!*

LITTLE RIDDLE

Nancy looked back up at Shelby's face.

Could she have been the kid in the sea monster costume? Was she at Deirdre's party after all?

"Shelby, what did you do today?" Nancy blurted.

"Nothing," Shelby blurted back. She started walking. "I've got to go now."

Nancy's head was spinning with questions as she watched Shelby walk up the block and turn the corner.

Could Shelby have been mad at Deirdre because she wasn't invited to Deirdre's sweet half-sixteen party? Did Shelby secretly crash Deirdre's party so she could throw the snake into Deirdre's pool?

"I don't want Shelby to be a suspect, Chip." Nancy sighed. "But it looks like she already is!"

"Woof!" Chip barked.

"Are you sure it was the same *pink* toenail polish the sea monster wore, Nancy?" Bess asked the next day as the Clue Crew headed to

Main Street. "There's cotton candy pink, hot pink, ballet pink—"

"It was pink, Bess!" Nancy cut in. "That's all I know."

"I just hope we find Shelby so we can ask her a few questions," George said.

"We will," Nancy assured her. "Shelby's mom told us she had an errand to run on Main Street."

It was Monday morning. It was also summer vacation, so the girls didn't have school. Instead they had all day to work on their case. The Clue Book was safely tucked inside Nancy's bag as she walked along. She had already added Shelby's name to the list of suspects:

1. ~~Crabby Carl's waiters~~
2. Taffy of Taffy's Topiaries
3. Sea monster
4. Shelby Metcalf

"Why would Shelby go to Deirdre's party if she wasn't invited?" Bess wondered.

"Maybe Shelby was mad at Deirdre for not inviting her," Nancy figured. "Mad enough to do something not-so-nice."

"You guys, look!" George said as they reached Main Street. She pointed at Yuks Joke Shop. Coiled in the store window was a green and yellow fake snake.

"That snake looks just like the ones at the party!" Nancy said. "Let's ask the owner if anyone bought a bunch of them lately."

A bell over the door jingled as Nancy, Bess, and George walked inside. Sitting behind a counter was a woman wearing a pirate bandana and an eye patch. On her Yuks T-shirt was a badge that read DEBBIE.

"Ahoy, me kiddies!" Debbie greeted in a pirate-like voice. "What brings you landlubbers to drop anchor at Yuks?"

"Snakes," Bess said.

"We would like to know who bought a bunch of fake snakes," Nancy explained. "Maybe you can tell us his or her name?"

"And not in pirate talk, please," George added. "This is serious business."

Debbie stared at the girls with her uncovered eye. She then shook her head.

"I can't give you that person's name," Debbie said. "But since this is a joke store I *can* give you a riddle."

"A riddle?" Nancy repeated.

"What's sweet, sticky, and really stretchy?" Debbie asked with a smile.

"Sweet?" Bess repeated.

"Sticky?" Nancy asked.

"Really stretchy?" George said.

The girls pondered the riddle. Then—

"Taffy!" the girls said at the same time.

They were about to high-five when the bell jingled again. Turning toward the door, they saw Shelby!

Shelby stared at Nancy, Bess, and George. Hanging from her hand was a Yuks shopping bag.

"Uh . . . I think I'm in the wrong store!" Shelby said, backing out of the door.

The girls thanked Debbie before following Shelby outside.

"Do you buy a lot of things at Yuks, Shelby?" Nancy asked her.

"What's in the bag, Shelby?" George asked.

"Library books," Shelby mumbled. "I have to return them so they're not overdue."

"When will they be overdue?" Bess asked.

"In five minutes!" Shelby said.

As Shelby dashed off, Nancy looked at the shopping bag in Shelby's hand. It didn't seem to be filled with books. Books would have made the bag look heavier than it did.

"Shelby will never tell us whether or not she was at Deirdre's party yesterday," Bess said.

"Oh yeah?" George said. "Watch this!"

The girls hurried to catch up with Shelby.

"Too bad you weren't at Deirdre's party, Shelby,"

George said. "Her parents surprised her with a real live dolphin named Marissa!"

"Dolphin?" Shelby said. She stopped walking. "You mean it was a *mermaid* named Mar—"

Shelby stopped mid-sentence. She clapped a hand over her mouth and mumbled, "Me and my big mouth."

"It's okay, Shelby," Nancy said gently. "How did you know it was a mermaid? Were you at Deirdre's party?"

Shelby didn't answer. Instead she began to run!

"Shelby!" Nancy shouted after her. "Please—wait up!"

SHELBY'S SECRET

Shelby was a superfast runner. Nancy, Bess, and George ran fast too, but they couldn't catch up.

"Shelby, we just want to ask you something!" Nancy called as they ran.

"I have nothing to say!" Shelby cried as she reached the end of the block. Just then a dog walker with six dogs came around the corner. Two dogs jumped up on Shelby, knocking the bag out of her hand.

"Oh no!" Shelby groaned as a glove and some other items fell out onto the sidewalk.

"I'm so sorry!" the dog walker said, tugging the pooches away from Shelby. As the dog walker and the dogs walked away, the Clue Crew raced over.

George pointed to the glove as well as other pieces of clothing scattered on the ground. "Hey!" she said. "That's the same sea monster costume we saw at the party yesterday."

"So?" Shelby said.

"So were you at Deirdre's party yesterday, Shelby?" Nancy asked nicely.

"We may be detectives, Shelby," Bess said with a little smile. "But we're still your friends. You can tell us."

Shelby cast her eyes downward and nodded.

"I *was* there," Shelby admitted. "Just now I was trying to return the costume I borrowed from Yuks. The one I wore to Deirdre's party."

"Why did you come if you weren't invited?" Bess asked.

"Because I didn't want to miss the best party ever!" Shelby wailed. "So I disguised myself and snuck in."

Nancy suddenly knew why Shelby wouldn't come into Deirdre's house. If Shelby had hung up her costume, everybody would have known it was her.

"What did you do while we all went into the house?" Nancy asked.

"I just hung around outside," Shelby said. "But I left after Queen Marissa showed up. My costume was crazy hot. I couldn't play games or talk to anyone, so I wasn't having fun."

"Did you really just hang around?" George asked. "Or did you throw that snake into Deirdre's pool?"

"Snake?" Shelby gasped. "What snake? Where? Where?"

Nancy was about to explain when Shelby began to shake all over.

"Oh no!" Shelby cried. "I hate snakes more than anything in the whole wide world!"

Shelby was still shaking as she began picking up her spilled costume.

"Shelby's really afraid of snakes," Nancy whispered as she, Bess, and George huddled a few feet away.

"She's got to be afraid of snakes to act like that," Bess murmured. "Unless she's just a good actress."

"No way," George whispered. "Remember when Shelby played Tinker Bell in the class play? She forgot almost all her lines!"

Nancy noticed one of the sea monster gloves

near their feet. Picking up the glove, Nancy studied it. The pointy sea monster fingers were webbed together almost like a duck's feet!

"Shelby couldn't have picked up a squirmy fake snake with fingers like these!" Nancy said, holding the sea monster glove. "She couldn't have thrown it into the pool either."

The Clue Crew walked back to Shelby.

"It was just a fake snake, Shelby," Nancy said, handing Shelby back the sea monster glove. "And we know you didn't throw it into Deirdre's pool."

Shelby gave a little smile.

"And guess what?" Bess said. "We're going to invite you to all our birthday parties from now on."

"Really?" Shelby asked.

"Sure!" Bess said. She smiled as she pointed to Shelby's feet. "As long as you let me borrow that awesome pink toenail polish!"

"Deal!" Shelby laughed.

The Clue Crew was happy that Shelby was no longer a suspect.

But as they were about to walk her back to Yuks—

VROOOOOOOM!!!!

Nancy, Bess, George, and Shelby whirled around. Speeding down the sidewalk on her fancy lavender electric scooter was Deirdre Shannon!

"Out of my waaaaaay!" Deirdre shouted from the scooter. "I can't stop this thing!!"

A-MAZE-ING!

Nancy, Bess, George, and Shelby jumped to the side.

"Step on the brake!" George shouted to Deirdre as she came zooming down the block. "Step on the brake, Deirdre!"

Deirdre screeched to a stop inches away from the girls. She took a deep breath, then removed her matching lavender helmet as if nothing had happened.

"Hi," Deirdre said. She looked directly at

Shelby. "Too bad you couldn't come to my perfect sweet half-sixteen party, Shelby."

"Yeah, too bad," Shelby said with a frown.

"Oh, but don't worry," Deirdre went on. "You can read all about my perfect sweet half-sixteen party on my famous blog, *Dishing with Deirdre*!"

Nancy rolled her eyes. Who at school *didn't* know the name of Deirdre's blog? She was the only eight-year-old kid in River Heights with one!

"I've got to go now," Shelby said. She gave Nancy, Bess, and George a quick wink. "To return my library books."

"See you, Shelby," Nancy said with a smile.

As Shelby walked away, Deirdre pulled her lavender-colored helmet back onto her head.

"I was just trying out my awesome new birthday present," Deirdre told the girls. "What were you doing?"

"As a matter of fact," George said, "we were looking for the person who threw the fake snake into your pool."

"Do you want to hear what we know so far,

Deirdre?" Nancy asked, pulling the Clue Book from her bag.

Deirdre shook her head. "I told you!" she groaned. "I don't care who did it. I just want to forget about it. My party was perfect, and that's all that counts."

"But Queen Marissa's water show was ruined because of the snake!" Bess said.

"*Queen* Marissa?" Deirdre cried. "There was only *one* queen at my party and that was me: Queen Deirdre of the Sea! So just let it go, okay?"

Deirdre flicked a switch on her scooter and

zoomed off. Nancy watched her zigzag down the block, and sighed.

"I don't get it," Nancy said. "Doesn't Deirdre want to know who tried to ruin her party?"

"Forget it, Nancy," George said. "Deirdre is too busy being queen!"

The girls walked down Main Street. Bess stopped at a popcorn cart to buy a bag of caramel corn. She shared some with Nancy and George as they continued on their way.

Nancy tapped the Clue Book with her pencil. "Our main suspect now is Taffy," she said, looking over the suspect list. She had already crossed Shelby and the sea monster off the list of suspects:

1. ~~Crabby Carl's waiters~~
2. Taffy of Taffy's Topiaries
3. ~~Sea monster~~
4. ~~Shelby Metcalf~~

"The woman in Yuks said that Taffy bought a bunch of fake snakes from the store," George said. "That's proof enough for me."

"But we don't know where Taffy is today," Bess said, munching on her popcorn. "How can we question her if we can't find her?"

George pulled an electronic tablet from her small backpack. "Ta-da!" she sang. "My mom let me borrow her mini tablet for the whole day!"

"Now we can look up where Taffy lives," Nancy said excitedly. "Thanks, George."

The Clue Crew sat on the bench while George did a search. She typed Taffy's name, then did her best to spell "topiaries."

Nancy and Bess peered over George's shoulder as Taffy's website appeared. The home page was filled with pictures of lovely green topiaries. It also showed Taffy's address.

"Taffy's gardening studio is only a few blocks away!" George said. "Let's go."

"Wait, George," Nancy said. "There's something else I want to look up."

"What?" George asked.

"Deirdre told us she wrote about her party in her blog," Nancy said. "Maybe she posted some pictures with clues too."

George found Deirdre's blog, *Dishing with Deirdre*. There were pictures of kids having fun at the party. There was even the picture of Deirdre and Queen Marissa.

Nancy studied the picture. The mermaid was smiling from ear to ear. Deirdre's hand was raised in a little wave.

"Why are Deirdre's hands so dirty in that picture?" Nancy pointed out.

"Maybe she was doing cartwheels on the grass before it was taken," Bess said with a shrug. "If I had a party like that, I'd be doing cartwheels too."

"I guess you're right," Nancy said. Still, something about the picture bothered her. Then, Nancy noticed something else.

"Why didn't Deirdre write about Queen Marissa on her blog?" Nancy asked.

George shrugged. "She probably didn't want to explain about the snake in the pool."

"It did ruin Marissa's big show, after all," Bess put in.

Nancy nodded. "That makes sense." She scribbled everything down in the Clue Book.

"Now let's find Taffy!" George declared.

Bess was still eating her popcorn when the girls reached Taffy's gardening studio. The gate was open so the girls walked inside. What they found was a garden filled with leafy green topiaries. There were topiaries of fish, birds—even cartoon characters.

But where was Taffy?

The girls were about to look for Taffy when Bess stopped at a tall hedge wall with an opening in the middle. A pebbly path led inside.

"There's probably a beautiful secret garden in there!" Bess said excitedly.

Before Nancy and George could stop her, Bess darted between the hedges and down the path.

"Bess, wait!" Nancy called. She could see Bess

racing down the walkway. "We'd better go after her, George."

"Yeah," George agreed. "If Taffy finds Bess snooping around, she might flip."

Nancy and George ran down the same path as Bess, but their friend had already disappeared.

"Where did she go?" Nancy wondered out loud.

Nancy and George were surrounded by tall, thick hedges. At the end of the path were two more paths. One led right, the other left.

"It's like walking through a big puzzle," Nancy said as they chose the left path. They were surrounded by hedges—and all the paths led this way and that.

"I think this is called a garden maze," George said. "I saw something about them on TV."

Nancy and George walked down the winding paths calling Bess's name.

"Where are you, Bess?" Nancy called.

"Come out, come out," George called, "wherever you are!"

"I'm over here!" Bess called back. She tossed a popcorn kernel in the air to show exactly where.

"There!" Nancy said, pointing to the flying popcorn. But when they took the nearest path to reach Bess she wasn't there.

"Something tells me Bess is lost." Nancy gulped.

"She's not the only one, Nancy," George said with a frown. "So are we!"

SNIP, SNIP, HOORAY!

Nancy and George ran up and down the shaded paths calling Bess's name. They were about to call for help when someone tapped Nancy's shoulder. Spinning around, she saw—

"Bess!" Nancy said happily.

"Let's get out of here," Bess said. She waved her hand in the opposite direction. "Follow me."

"How do you know the way out?" George asked.

Bess held up her bag of popcorn and smiled.

"There was a hole in the bottom of my popcorn

bag," Bess explained. "I've been spilling popcorn on the ground by accident!"

"So you left a popcorn trail!" George declared. "Good work, Bess—even though you didn't mean it."

"Shouldn't we pick up the popcorn along the way?" Nancy asked. "We don't want to litter."

"The birds will eat the popcorn," Bess explained. "I just hope they like crunchy caramel corn!"

Nancy, Bess, and George followed the popcorn trail through the maze until they saw sunlight at the end of the path.

"We're out of here!" George declared.

The girls raced toward the opening. As they burst out of the maze, they saw Taffy. The garden designer looked surprised to see Nancy, Bess, and George.

"Uh . . . hi, Taffy," Nancy said.

"We were just checking out your amazing maze," Bess said.

"I can see that!" Taffy said. "I would have preferred you go inside with a grown-up, but I'm glad you didn't get lost."

"Lost? Us? No way!" George scoffed until Nancy gave her an elbow-nudge.

"Do you make mazes too, Taffy?" Bess asked.

"Just this one," Taffy answered. "I've worked on it for years."

Taffy then tilted her head and said, "Weren't you girls at the sweet half-sixteen party yesterday?"

"Yes," Nancy replied.

"So . . . what are you doing here?" Taffy asked.

"Someone put a rubber snake in the Shannons' pool," Bess explained. "We want to find out who did it."

"And you think it's me?" Taffy asked surprised.

"We did find two fake snakes around your topiaries yesterday," Nancy said. "They looked exactly like the snake in the pool!"

"Only two snakes?" Taffy said, tapping her chin thoughtfully. "I could have sworn I put down three."

The Clue Crew stared at Taffy. If this was a confession, it was the easiest one yet!

"So you *did* bring the fake snakes to Deirdre's party?" Nancy asked.

"How come?" George asked.

"Was it to scare Deirdre?" Bess asked.

Taffy laughed as she shook her head.

"I often use fake snakes to keep squirrels and other critters away from my topiaries," Taffy said. "It's a trick lots of gardeners use."

"A trick?" Nancy repeated.

"Most small critters don't like snakes very much," Taffy explained. "They don't know my snakes are fake, so they run away!"

"Queen Marissa didn't know the snakes were fake either," Bess said. "The one in the pool scared the mermaid away from Deirdre's party!"

Taffy shook her head and said, "That may have been my snake, but I never threw it into the pool."

"But you said you were going to surprise Deirdre," Nancy said.

"Not like that!" Taffy insisted. An excited smile spread across her face. "Would you like to see what my surprise *really* is?"

Nancy, Bess, and George traded curious looks. What could it be? They followed Taffy to where her topiaries stood. Taffy pointed to one. It was trimmed to look like a girl wearing a leafy green crown.

"Presenting Deirdre Shannon!" Taffy declared. "Queen of the Sea!"

The girls stared up at the topiary. It was what Deirdre had wanted so badly. It was a topiary of herself!

While Taffy admired her own work, the Clue Crew whispered about the case. Nancy pulled out the Clue Book and pencil and drew a big line through Taffy's name:

1. ~~Crabby Carl's waiters~~
2. ~~Taffy of Taffy's Topiaries~~
3. ~~Sea monster~~
4. ~~Shelby Metcalf~~

"So that was Taffy's surprise," Bess whispered. "Not the snake in the pool."

"But it was Taffy's fake snake," Nancy said quietly. "If Taffy didn't do it, someone else must have wanted Marissa out of there!"

"How could anyone not like Marissa?" Bess asked. "She's Queen of the Mermaids!"

"I don't know," George said. "But someone got their hands on Taffy's snakes!"

Hands? The word gave Nancy an idea!

She turned to Taffy and asked, "Did the Shannons know about your fake snakes?"

"Of course," Taffy answered. "I needed to make sure the fake snakes were okay with them."

Nancy stared at Taffy. Then she examined the Clue Book. She looked at all the clues and suspects. That's when things began to click!

Nancy turned to her friends. "I know who did it," she whispered. "I know who threw the snake into Deirdre's pool!"

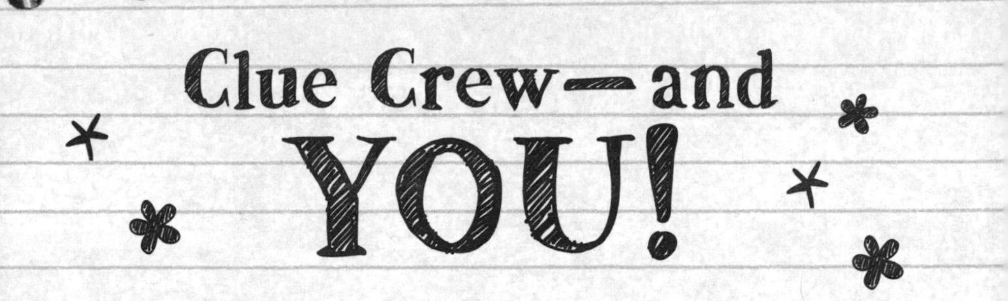

Clue Crew—and YOU!

Can you solve the Pool Party Puzzler? Write your answers on a sheet of paper. Or just turn the page to find out!

First, list your suspects.

Next, write down the name of the fake snake slinger.

What clues helped you to solve this mystery?

MESS UP, FESS UP!

"It was Deirdre!" Nancy announced.

"How do you know that?" Bess asked.

"Because Deirdre knew about Taffy's snakes," Nancy explained. "Plus, she had dirt on her hands in that picture we looked at. And I'm pretty sure it wasn't from cartwheels."

"It was from picking up a snake in the grass," Bess said, her blue eyes wide.

"And Deirdre didn't even act excited about Queen Marissa," Nancy added. "She didn't even write about her in her blog."

"And she seemed really mad when I called Marissa a queen," Bess recalled.

"Because Deirdre always has to be queen of everything!" George groaned.

"It all fits together," Bess said. "But there's only one way to know for sure. Let's find Deirdre and ask her!"

Nancy, Bess, and George made sure to thank Taffy before they left.

"You're welcome," Taffy said. She then pointed to a flock of birds flying into her maze. "I guess birds really like my maze too."

"Or caramel popcorn!" Bess giggled.

The girls left Taffy's studio and headed straight for Deirdre's house.

"No wonder Deirdre didn't want us to work on the case," George said on the way. "She was trying to hide the fact that she was the snake slinger!"

When the Clue Crew reached the Shannons' house they found Deirdre in her backyard. She was busily taking pictures of her birthday presents. Her new electric scooter stood in the middle of them all.

"Hi, Deirdre," Nancy said.

"What are you doing?" George asked.

"My mom wants me to write thank-you cards," Deirdre said, rolling her eyes. "I'm going to write one thank-you on my blog instead—with a picture of all my presents!"

Deirdre held the camera up to take a selfie with her presents in the background. As she flashed a big smile, Nancy asked the big question.

"Deirdre? Did you throw that fake snake in your pool yesterday?"

Deirdre's smile turned into a frown. "Why would I want to ruin my own party?" Deirdre demanded.

"Maybe because you wanted to make sure there wasn't another queen at your party," Nancy said slowly. "So you threw a fake snake in the pool before Marissa could swim."

"Marissa told everyone she'd be swimming," George added. "What better way to scare her away?"

Deirdre stared openmouthed at the Clue Crew.

She then shook her head from side to side.

"That is totally silly," Deirdre insisted. "I never threw Taffy's snake in the pool—"

"We never said it was Taffy's snake," Bess cut in with a smile. "How did you know?"

Deirdre opened her mouth to speak, but nothing came out. Finally she groaned and said, "Why did I ever invite the Clue Crew to my party?"

"Does that mean you did it, Deirdre?" Nancy asked.

"If so, why?" Bess asked.

"Because I didn't want another queen at my party," Deirdre admitted. "I remembered Taffy's snakes and decided to have some fun."

"It wasn't fun for Marissa," Nancy said. "You ruined her show *and* your party."

"My party?" Deirdre gasped. "My party wasn't ruined!"

"But everyone wanted to see Marissa swim," Bess said. "Now we'll never get to."

"You also blamed your friends for what you did," George added. "Not cool."

"So my party wasn't *perfect*?" Deirdre cried.

"It could have been," Nancy said, "if it wasn't for that icky fake snake."

"Phooey," Deirdre muttered under her breath.

"And after you write your thank-you note, Deirdre," Nancy said. "You should write something *else* in your blog."

"Something else?" Deirdre asked, wrinkling her nose. "What?"

"An apology!" Nancy declared.

The Clue Crew left Deirdre alone in her yard. They were happy they had solved the case and just as happy that summer vacation had begun.

"Now that we solved our first case of the summer," George said, "what should we do next?"

"I know!" Nancy said excitedly, carefully placing the Clue Book into her bag. "Let's have our own sweet half-sixteen parties."

"And be queens too?" Bess asked.

"Sure!" Nancy said with a smile. "Queens of mysteries!"

Last Lemonade Standing

Chapter 1

SOUR POWER

"I don't get it," eight-year-old Nancy Drew said. "Doesn't anyone want lemonade?"

Nancy sat with her two best friends behind their lemonade stand. The table holding a pitcher of lemonade and paper cups was set up in the Drews' front yard.

"Maybe it's too hot," Bess Marvin suggested.

"We're selling ice-cold lemonade, Bess," George Fayne groaned. "Not hot cocoa!"

Nancy counted the few quarters and dimes

in a glass jar. She then wrote the total on her favorite writing pad with the ladybug design.

"At the rate we're going," Nancy said with a sigh, "we'll never earn enough money to buy Katy Sloan tickets."

Bess and George sighed too. Katy Sloan was their favorite singer. When they had heard that Katy's next concert would be at the River Heights Amusement Park, they knew they had to go. But Nancy, Bess, and George had already gone to the amusement park twice that summer to ride the rides. Both times their parents had paid for the tickets. So they would have to buy these tickets with their own money.

That's when Nancy had the idea for a lemonade stand. They even taped a picture of Katy to the table to make them work harder! Bess had written the date of the concert right on it.

"We've been selling lemonade for two whole days," Nancy said.

"And I know our lemonade is good enough," Bess insisted. "I got the recipe from my Pixie Scout cookbook!"

"Maybe that's the problem, Bess," George said. "Sometimes good enough isn't enough."

Nancy glanced over her shoulder at her house.

"If only Hannah would give us her top-secret recipe for pink-strawberry lemonade," Nancy said. "It's awesome!"

"Top secret?" Bess said, her blue eyes wide.

"Even from you?" George asked Nancy. "Hannah has been your housekeeper since you were four years old."

"*Three* years old!" Nancy corrected. "And Hannah is more than a housekeeper—she's like a mother to me."

"Then why won't she give you her recipe?" Bess asked.

"I told you, it's top secret!" Nancy said. She flashed a little smile. "Even from detectives like us!"

When Nancy, Bess, and George weren't selling lemonade they were part of a detective club called the Clue Crew. Nancy even had a special Clue Book so she could write down clues and suspects.

"Speaking of detective stuff," George said with a smile. "I joined the Spy Girl Gadget of the Month Club."

"You joined a club without us?" Bess gasped. "But Nancy is your best friend—and I'm your best cousin!"

"Are you *sure* you two are cousins?" Nancy joked.

Bess and George *were* cousins, but totally different.

Bess had blond hair, blue eyes, and a closet full of fashion-forward clothes. George had dark hair and eyes and liked her nickname better than her real name, Georgia. George's closet was full too—with electronic gadgets!

"The Spy Girl Gadget of the Month Club isn't really a club, Bess," George explained. "I just get a new spy gadget in the mail once a month."

George held up a purple pen and said, "The first gadget came yesterday. It's called a Presto Pen."

"What does it do?" Nancy asked.

"I don't know," George admitted. "I think my little brother, Scott, took the instructions—just like he takes everything else that belongs to me—"

"You guys, look!" Bess interrupted.

Nancy turned to see where Bess was pointing. Walking toward their lemonade stand were Andrea Wu, Bobby Wozniak, and Ben Washington from their third-grade class at school.

"Customers!" Nancy said. She smoothed her reddish-blond hair with her hands and whispered, "Everybody, smile!"

The kids approached, each wearing a *READY, SET, COOK!* T-shirt.

"'Ready, set, cook,'" Nancy read out loud. "Isn't that the kids' cooking show on TV?"

"Exactly!" Andrea said proudly. "You're looking at one of the next teams on the show—Team Lollipop!"

"Neat!" Bess said. "What are you going to cook?"

"Our challenge is to put together a picnic basket," Ben explained. "We're making chicken salad on rolls, potato salad, crunchy coleslaw, and pecan bars."

Nancy was surprised to see Bobby on the team. Bobby's nickname was Buggy because he loved bugs!

"You like to cook, Buggy?" Nancy asked.

"Not really," Bobby said. "My mom made me join the cooking show so I'd stop thinking about bugs this summer."

"How about some lemonade?" Bess asked.

"I'd rather have bug juice!" Buggy sighed.

"I'll have a cup, please," Ben said with a smile.

"One cup coming up!" George said. She picked up the pitcher and carefully poured lemonade into a paper cup. Ben drank it in one gulp.

"Not bad," Ben said, smacking his lips. "I taste lemons, sugar, water, and a small dash of vanilla extract."

"You tasted all that?" Nancy exclaimed.

"I can taste anything and name each ingredient!" Ben said proudly. "Superheroes have X-ray vision, but I have X-ray taste buds."

"Wow!" George said. She offered Andrea a cup, but she shook her head.

"No, thanks," Andrea said. "I just had a cup at Lily Ramos's lemonade stand."

Nancy, Bess, and George knew Lily from school. They also knew that Lily's Aunt Maria owned a chain of famous coffee-and-tea cafés called Beans and Bags.

"What's Lily's lemonade like?" Nancy asked.

"Pretty sour," Andrea said, scrunching her nose. "But her lemonade stand rocks!"

The girls traded surprised looks as Team Lollipop walked away.

"What could be so special about Lily's lemonade stand?" Bess wondered.

"There's only one way to find out," Nancy said. "Let's go over to Lily's house and check it out."

Nancy wrote BE RIGHT BACK on her ladybug pad. After putting the lemonade pitcher in the kitchen fridge, the girls made their way to Lily Ramos's house two blocks away.

Nancy, Bess, and George each had the same rule: They could walk anywhere as long as it wasn't more than five blocks away and as long as they were together. They didn't mind. Being together was more fun anyway!

"Whoa!" George gasped when they reached the Ramoses' front yard.

Behind Lily's lemonade stand were cushy chairs and a rolling book cart for customers.

There were board games on tiny tables and a FREE WI-FI sign.

When Lily saw Nancy, Bess, and George, she smiled.

"*This* is your lemonade stand, Lily?" Nancy asked.

"I like to call it a lemonade *experience*!"

Lily said. "My aunt Maria told me exactly what to do."

As Lily gave the girls a tour of her yard, she said, "It's also pet friendly . . . and for your sipping pleasure, my cousin Carlos will play his recorder!"

Nancy watched as Lily's six-year-old cousin strolled by, playing "Twinkle, Twinkle, Little Star." She then noticed something else. The prices of the lemonade, cupcakes, and cookies were written on the same ladybug paper she owned.

"Andrea was right," Nancy whispered to Bess and George. "Lily's lemonade stand really does rock."

But when they tried Lily's lemonade, their faces puckered up. Andrea was right about something else—Lily's lemonade was too sour!

"Don't you like it?" Lily asked.

"Um . . . it just needs a little something," Nancy said nicely.

"Like magic!" George joked.

"It's just that we have a lemonade stand too, Lily!" Bess said quickly.

"And your lemonade is better than mine?" Lily cried.

"Not better," Nancy said slowly. "Just . . . different."

Lily was still frowning as she left to help a customer. But as the girls walked out of Lily's yard, they were frowning too.

"No wonder we have no customers," Nancy said. "All the kids in River Heights are going to Lily's lemonade stand."

"You mean lemonade *experience*," George said. "Nobody seems to care that the lemonade tastes like swamp water."

"How are we going to sell enough lemonade for Katy Sloan tickets," Bess asked, "when everyone is buying from Lily?"

Nancy gave it some thought. There was only one way to bring customers to their lemonade stand.

"We need the most awesome lemonade

in the whole world, that's how!" Nancy announced.

"Where are we going to find that?" Bess wondered.

"By asking Hannah," Nancy said with a smile, "for her top-secret recipe for pink-strawberry lemonade!"

Chapter 2

TOP SECRET!

"Please, Hannah?" Nancy said. "Pretty please with sugar on top . . . and a strawberry?"

"Why don't I make the lemonade for you?" Hannah suggested. "Without telling you the recipe?"

"Thanks, Hannah," Nancy said. "But we really want to make our own lemonade for our own lemonade stand!"

The girls held their breaths while Hannah thought. Would she finally reveal the secret

Gruen family recipe for pink-strawberry lemonade?

"Everyone in my family had to promise to keep our recipe secret," Hannah said. "So you have to promise too!"

"Does that mean yes?" Nancy gasped.

"Only if you promise," Hannah said.

"We promise!" Nancy, Bess, and George said together.

"Okay then," Hannah said. "Grab a pen and paper and write down the ingredients."

Nancy remembered her ladybug notepad in her pocket. But when she looked around for a pen, she couldn't find one.

"Use this," George said. She handed Nancy her Presto Pen.

"Thanks, George," Nancy said. She then stood behind the kitchen counter ready to write the secret ingredients.

Hannah paced back and forth calling out the ingredients: lemons, strawberries, crushed mint leaves, both flat water and fizzy water to give it a little zip. . . .

"And last but not least," Hannah said, "two tablespoons of honey instead of sugar. That's what makes it special."

Nancy carefully wrote the ingredients and measurements. When she was done, she looked up and said, "Thanks a million, Hannah!"

After giving Hannah a big hug, Nancy ran to the calendar on the kitchen wall. She drew a heart around the date of Katy Sloan's concert—four days away. Would it be enough time to earn ticket money?

"Katy Sloan concert, here we come!" Nancy declared. She was about to return the Presto Pen when George shook her head.

"Keep the Presto Pen for

now, Nancy," George said. "Maybe it'll bring us good luck."

The girls walked together to the supermarket for lemonade ingredients. Once there they used two shopping carts. Since the recipe was top secret, they didn't want anyone to see all of the ingredients in one cart. They even spoke in secret code.

"Do we have enough aw-berries-stray?" Nancy whispered.

"Four baskets of aw-berries-stray," Bess said.

"On to the oney-hey," George whispered.

"The what?" Bess asked.

"The honey, Bess!" George said.

"Shhh!" Nancy hissed. "It's top secret!"

Nancy and George pushed both carts up the aisle. Bess pointed to a shelf with lemon-shaped jars. They were filled with Lickety-Split instant-lemonade powder.

"Look," Bess said. "Lickety-Split makes pink-strawberry lemonade, too!"

"It can't be as good as ours," Nancy said as

she held up Hannah's recipe. "That's a mix and ours is fresh."

Then as the girls walked under a whirling ceiling fan—*whoosh*—the wind blew the recipe out of Nancy's hand!

"Hannah's recipe!" Nancy cried as the paper shot up the aisle. "We have to get it before someone sees it!"

"But we can't leave our carts!" George said. "Or someone will see the ingredients!"

Pushing their carts, the girls chased the flyaway recipe until a boy stepped out from behind a tower of cereal boxes. It was Henderson "Drippy" Murphy from school.

Henderson's dad was Mr. Drippy the ice-cream man. Mr. Drippy's truck was a huge part of summer in River Heights.

"What's this?" Henderson asked, picking up the recipe.

George snatched the recipe from his hand and said, "It's our shopping list. No biggie."

"Whatever," Henderson said with a shrug.

He was wearing a T-shirt with Katy Sloan's picture on the front!

"Do you like Katy Sloan too?" Nancy asked.

"I don't like *her*," Henderson said, his cheeks blushing. "I just like her music, that's all."

Henderson then pointed to the lemons in one of the shopping carts. "But I *hate* lemons!" he said angrily.

"Why?" Bess asked.

"My dad traded his ice-cream truck for a dumb lemonade shake-up truck," Henderson explained. "What's so special about lemonade anyway?"

"*Our* lemonade will be special!" Bess blurted excitedly. "We're making pink—"

George clapped her hand over Bess's mouth before she could say more. Henderson shrugged again, then walked away.

"You almost spilled our secret, Bess!" George said.

"But she didn't!" Nancy said with a smile. "Now let's find the rest of the ingredients and get to work."

Nancy, Bess, and George spent the rest of the day squeezing lemons, blending strawberries, and measuring honey. By dinnertime they had three pitchers of Hannah's pink-strawberry lemonade. The girls each took a test-sip. . . .

"Yum!" George said.

"Yummy!" Nancy added.

"Yummy for the tummy!" Bess exclaimed.

The girls traded high fives. Their lemonade

was awesome. Hopefully their customers tomorrow would think so too!

"You guys," Nancy said excitedly the next morning. "We're lemonade superstars!"

Nancy still couldn't believe it as she poured another cup of cold pink-strawberry lemonade. They had set up their stand just an hour ago, and they already had served ten customers!

"Giving out samples of our lemonade was a great idea, George," Nancy said as more kids lined up. "Everybody is coming back for more."

"With their friends!" Bess pointed out.

Nancy had remembered to tape their picture of Katy Sloan on the table next to the iced sugar cookies that Hannah had baked for them to sell. She was about to brush away some crumbs when one more customer stepped up to the table. . . .

"Lily!" Nancy said with surprise. "Why aren't you at your own lemonade stand—I mean, lemonade experience?"

"I heard your lemonade is awesome," Lily said. She bought a cup, took a sip, and gasped. "This *is* awesome. How did you make it?"

"Sorry," George said. "Our lips are zipped."

Lily frowned before walking away. Nancy had no time to wonder if Lily was jealous. They had thirsty kids to feed!

"What if we run out of lemonade?" Bess asked.

"I still have the recipe if we need to make more," Nancy said, holding up her ladybug paper. "Can you put it in your messenger bag so it's safe, Bess?"

Bess took the recipe just as a bunch of kids walked over. This time it was Henderson followed by Team Lollipop.

"I'll get more cups!" George said happily. As she ran back to the house, Henderson stepped up to the stand.

"I heard your lemonade rocks," Henderson said. He nodded at the pitcher. "But why is it pink?"

"It's pink-strawberry lemonade!" Nancy said proudly.

"Strawberry?" Henderson cried his eyes wide. "Nobody told me it was *strawberry* lemonade!"

Nancy and Bess were surprised too. What was Henderson's problem? But then—

"We're in a hurry," Andrea said as she stepped in front of Henderson. "We have to be at the TV studio soon. *Ready, Set, Cook!* starts filming at three o'clock!"

"And we're going to win the summer picnic-basket contest!" Ben added excitedly.

George hurried back, her arms overflowing with more paper cups. Bess took three and began to pour.

"Three cups, coming up!" Bess declared.

Andrea and Buggy sipped their lemonade first. They thought it was the best ever. Bess was about to pour Ben's cup when George shook her head.

"Don't, Bess!" George whispered. "If Ben tastes our lemonade, he'll know the secret ingredients!"

"Ben has X-ray taste buds!" Nancy added.

"Um . . . what's up?" Ben asked.

The girls traded looks. They had to keep Ben from tasting their secret strawberry lemonade—but how?

"Uh . . . I . . . just saw a bug inside the pitcher," Nancy said, thinking fast. "No more lemonade until we get it out."

"A bug?" Buggy said excitedly. "What kind? Where?"

In a flash Buggy reached out, knocking the pitcher and plate of cookies off the table.

"Now I'll never get to see the bugs!" Buggy pouted.

Bess and George groaned as the last of the lemonade trickled onto the grass. But Nancy was more worried about the cookies. Some of them had chocolate icing on top. What if her puppy, Chocolate Chip, ate them? Chocolate was dangerous for dogs to eat.

"Pick up the cookies!" Nancy said. "Before Chip finds them!"

Nancy, Bess, and George bent down to pick up the cookies. By the time they stood up, Team Lollipop was gone. Walking away from the stand was Henderson, stuffing something into his pocket.

"We can make more lemonade, Henderson!" Nancy called.

"No, thanks!" Henderson called back.

Nancy watched as Henderson hurried out

of the yard and up the block. What was his rush? Suddenly—

"Omigosh!" Bess cried. "I put Hannah's recipe here on the table before I poured the lemonade. And now . . . and now . . ."

Nancy stared at Bess. Her heart began to pound as she thought the worst.

"Hannah's recipe is gone?" Nancy cried.

"Well, yes . . . and no," Bess said. She held up the ladybug paper. "The paper is still here . . . but the *recipe* is gone!"

RECIPE FOR TROUBLE

Nancy, Bess, and George stared at the ladybug paper. It was totally blank!

"What happened to Hannah's recipe?" Nancy exclaimed.

"Maybe someone switched the recipe with the same ladybug paper," George suggested. "A blank piece of ladybug paper!"

"That means Hannah's secret recipe for pink-strawberry lemonade was *stolen*!" Nancy gasped.

"And it's my fault!" Bess cried. "I was going to put the recipe in my bag, but when things got busy I forgot!"

Nancy shook her head and said, "It's my fault. I should never have taken Hannah's recipe out of my pocket!"

"Who cares whose fault it is?" George said. "Nancy, how are you going to tell Hannah her top-secret lemonade recipe was stolen?"

Nancy's stomach did a double flip. Could she really tell Hannah that her recipe was stolen after they had promised to keep it a secret?

"We can't tell Hannah!" Nancy blurted. "Not until I find the person who took the recipe."

"Why, Nancy?" Bess asked slowly. "Whoever took the recipe already knows the secret ingredients."

"I know," Nancy said sadly. "But maybe the recipe thief will promise to keep it a secret too."

"It's worth a try," George said.

Nancy nodded and said, "The Clue Book

is in my room. Let's clean up here, then get to work."

"The Clue Book?" George said with a grin. "I know what that means."

"So do I," Bess said. "It means the Clue Crew is on the case!"

Nancy, Bess, and George carried their lemonade stand supplies into the kitchen.

"Closing your stand so soon?" Hannah asked, surprised. "Didn't the kids like my top-secret lemonade recipe?"

The girls traded looks. What would they tell Hannah?

"Um—the kids loved it, Hannah!" Nancy said. "But then . . . then . . ."

"It got too hot for lemonade!" George piped in.

"How could it be too hot for ice-cold lemonade?" Hannah asked.

"If all our ice melted?" Bess blurted.

The girls left the kitchen and hurried up the stairs. Nancy felt awful for not telling Hannah the truth. But she couldn't—not yet!

Once they were in Nancy's room, the girls huddled around the Clue Book. Nancy opened it to a clean page. Then, using the pen George lent her, she wrote the name of their new case:

Who Took Hannah's Top-Secret Recipe
for Pink-Strawberry Lemonade?

Underneath that, she wrote:

Suspects.

"It's got to be Henderson 'Drippy' Murphy," George said. "I saw him stuff something inside his pocket when he left our lemonade stand."

"I saw it too," Nancy said.

"I saw it three!" Bess added.

"Did you also see how weird Henderson acted when he found out that our lemonade was strawberry-flavored?" Nancy asked.

"Maybe Henderson wanted a pink-strawberry recipe for his dad's lemonade truck," Bess suggested. "But what would he be doing with ladybug paper?"

Nancy thought hard. Maybe the recipe thief didn't switch the ladybug papers.

"Maybe I accidentally wrote the recipe on two pieces of ladybug paper stuck together," Nancy explained. "Henderson could have taken the top sheet, leaving a blank one underneath."

Nancy wrote Henderson's name in the Clue Book. His was the first name on her suspect list.

Henderson

"The Clue Crew has a suspect!" George said with a grin. "Sweet!"

Bess's eyes popped wide open. "George, did you say 'sweet'?" she asked.

"Yeah, so?" George said.

"Sweet makes me think of Team Lollipop!" Bess said excitedly. "They were at our stand right before the recipe went missing."

"Team Lollipop could have taken the recipe while we were picking up the cookies," George said with a nod.

"Buggy probably has ladybug paper too!" Bess added. She wrinkled her nose. "Anything to do with bugs!"

But Nancy wasn't too sure about Team Lollipop.

"Why would Team Lollipop want our lemonade recipe?" Nancy asked. "It's not like they have a lemonade stand."

"Lily Ramos has a lemonade stand," George said. "And she has the exact same ladybug paper, too."

"But Lily left right after she tasted our lemonade," Bess said.

"Lily could have hid somewhere," George said. "To secretly snoop on us and our lemonade stand."

"Lily said our lemonade was awesome," Nancy added. "Maybe she wanted the recipe for her own lemonade stand!"

"You mean lemonade *experience*!" Bess giggled.

Nancy added Lily's name to their suspect list.

Lily

She then shut the Clue Book and said, "Let's go outside and see if we can find some clues."

The three girls slipped past Hannah and out the front door. The table they had used for their lemonade stand was still in the front yard.

"Our picture of Katy Sloan is gone," Bess noticed, pointing to the table.

"The wind probably blew it away," George said. "I should have used more tape."

Nancy spotted a piece of paper on the grass. It wasn't their picture of Katy—it looked like some kind of list.

Nancy picked up the paper and studied it.

"Bess, George," Nancy said. "This is a list of the food that's going into Team Lollipop's picnic basket!"

"You mean for the TV show *Ready, Set, Cook!*?" Bess asked.

"It must be what Andrea put on the table when she paid for her lemonade," George said. "So what's cookin'?"

"Yummy stuff!" Nancy said as she smiled down at the list. "There's chicken salad on rolls, crunchy coleslaw, potato salad, lemonade—"

Nancy stopped midsentence. Did she just see what she thought she saw?

Was Team Lollipop making *lemonade*?

COOKS . . . OR CROOKS?

The Clue Crew huddled around Team Lollipop's list. At the end *was* the word "lemonade"!

"They didn't say they were making lemonade yesterday," Nancy said.

"They're making it now!" George said. "What better way to win a cooking contest than with the best pink-strawberry lemonade recipe in the world?"

"How do we know it's Hannah's recipe?" Bess asked.

Nancy knew how they could find out. She looked at her watch. It was one thirty.

"Andrea said that the contest starts filming at three o'clock," Nancy said. "We should go to the TV station too."

"But we're not on a team!" Bess said. "They'll never let us in!"

"My mom is a caterer and works with lots of chefs," George said, her eyes lighting up. "Chefs mean chefs' *hats*!"

"Chefs' hats, huh?" Nancy repeated slowly. "I like it. I like it."

The Clue Crew was about to go undercover!

"How do people cook with these things on?" Bess complained an hour later. "This hat keeps flopping in my face!"

"They're chefs' hats for grown-ups, Bess," George said. "So *grow up* and quit complaining!"

Nancy carried a wicker picnic basket as the Clue Crew approached Station WRIV-TV. After filing through the front door, the girls were greeted by a guard. Her last name was embroidered on her jacket: BROWN.

"Can I help you?" Ms. Brown asked from behind her desk.

"We're here for the *Ready, Set, Cook!* show," Nancy said, flashing a big smile.

"That's why we're dressed like chefs!" Bess explained.

Ms. Brown raised an eyebrow and said, "And what's the name of your team?"

"Um—Team Broccoli!" George blurted.

"Ew—not broccoli, George!" Bess cried. She smiled at Ms. Brown and said, "It's Team Cupcake!"

"I happen to like broccoli, Bess!" George hissed. But Ms. Brown wasn't buying it one bit.

"If you're Team Cupcake," Ms. Brown said. "Why do your hats read 'Louise Fayne Catering'?"

Gulp! Nancy, Bess, and George rolled their eyes up to their hats. They hadn't thought of that!

"Because . . . it's good advertising for my mom?" George said. "She's a caterer."

Bess stepped forward. She pointed to the picnic basket in Nancy's hand.

"Excuse me, Ms. Brown," Bess said. "We have ice cream in here. If we don't get to the studio soon, you'll have a mint chocolate-chip puddle on your floor!"

Nancy tried not to giggle. Their basket was really empty—but Bess's idea seemed to be working!

"Okay, okay," Ms. Brown said pointing down a long hallway. "*Ready, Set, Cook!* is shot in Studio B."

"Thank you!" Bess said sweetly.

Nancy, Bess, and George raced down the hall to the door marked Studio B. But when they stepped inside the studio, it was dark and empty.

"Where is everybody?" Nancy asked.

There were TV cameras, lights hanging from the ceiling, and three big, shiny cooking counters. But no people!

"It's better empty," George said. "Now we can look for clues without anyone knowing."

The Clue Crew headed straight for the cooking counters. Each one had a sign reading one of the names of the three teams.

"'Team Popsicle,' 'Team Pepperoni,'" Bess read out loud. "And 'Team Lollipop'!"

Nancy, Bess, and George ran to Team Lollipop's cooking counter. It was big enough to hold the cooking ingredients for the contest plus mixing bowls and spoons of all sizes.

"Here's a bowl of lemons," Nancy said, picking up the bowl. "Now we *know* they're making lemonade!"

"Check it out!" George said. She reached under the counter to pull a square plastic container off a shelf. Written on the lid were the words "Top Secret!"

"Top secret?" Nancy said. She put down the bowl to look at the container. "Why would it say that?"

"Maybe it's Hannah's recipe!" Bess said excitedly. "It's so good they don't want anyone else to know what's in it!"

"I'm opening it!" George said. But just as she was about to pop the lid—

FLASH!

Nancy, Bess, and George jumped as the huge lights suddenly came on all at once.

"I hear voices outside the door!" George whispered. "Somebody is coming!"

The girls didn't want anyone to know they

were snooping. So they ducked under the counter seconds before the studio door swung open. The counter was big enough to hide all three girls and their basket underneath.

Carefully, the girls peeked out. They could see people filing through the door into the studio. They were grown-ups wearing headsets, a man dressed in a jacket and tie, and the three cooking teams.

"The guy in a jacket is the host of the show," Nancy whispered. "His name is Gordon Whimsy."

"I know," Bess whispered. "He's strict with the teams!"

"But he's an awesome cook," George whispered, the top-secret container clutched in her hand.

One woman began calling out orders to the crew. Nancy guessed she was the director of *Ready, Set, Cook!*

"Okay, people!" the woman shouted. "That last-minute tech meeting put us all behind schedule, so everybody get in their places so we can start shooting the contest!"

"Sure, Ellen!" the stage manager said with a smile.

But Gordon wasn't smiling as he groaned, "Delays, delays. Nothing but delays!"

The girls froze as three pairs of legs appeared outside the counter. It was Team Lollipop, ready to cook!

"Hey!" Andrea said. "That's not where I put the lemon bowl."

"And where's my secret box?" Buggy said.

"What secret box?" Ben asked.

"Um . . . nothing," Buggy replied.

Nancy, Bess, and George traded puzzled looks under the counter. Did only Buggy know about the box?

"Quiet, everyone, please!" the stage manager shouted before counting down. "Three . . . two . . . one!"

The show's opening tune blasted through the studio. After that the voice of an announcer boomed: "Hey, let's get cooking, kids, because it's time for—"

"READY! SET! COOK!" the three teams yelled out.

Nancy, Bess, and George peeked out to see Gordon smiling straight at the camera.

"I'm your host, Gordon Whimsy," Gordon said cheerily. "Now that you've met me, let's meet our cooking-good teams!"

From the corner of her eye Nancy saw George fumbling with the secret box.

"What are you doing?" Nancy whispered.

"Trying to open this secret box!" George whispered. "If the recipe is inside, I want to know!"

The box popped open. George stared

into it. She then sucked her breath in softly.

"Is it our recipe, George?" Bess whispered.

"Nope," George whispered back.

"What is it?" Nancy whispered.

"It's . . . ants!" George gulped.

5

GETTING ANTSY

"Ants?" Nancy hissed. She, Bess, and George peered inside the container. It *was* filled with ants. About a dozen of them!

"Gross!" Bess hissed. "Close the lid—quick!"

Bess reached out to shut the container. Instead she knocked the container out of George's hand. It fell on the floor with a *plunk*, spilling the creepy-crawly ants onto the floor!

An army of ants crawled straight toward Team Lollipop's feet just as they were being interviewed by Gordon Whimsy!

"And here's a team that's hard to lick—Team Lollipop!" Gordon announced. "Kids, what will be in your picnic basket today?"

"Ants!" Andrea screamed.

"Pardon me?" Gordon asked.

"I've got ants crawling up my leg!" Andrea shouted.

"And I've got ants up my pants!" Ben cried.

The girls crawled out from under the table—before the rest of the ants could crawl all over them!

"Nancy? Bess? George?" Andrea cried, shaking her leg. "What are you doing here?"

Nancy was about to explain when Ellen the director charged out of the control room.

"I said, 'Cut!'" Ellen cried. "I want to know how those ants got into this studio!"

Nancy knew they had to tell the truth.

"They were in a box marked top secret," Nancy explained. "George opened it while we were hiding under the table."

"Why were you hiding under the table?" Ellen asked.

"We're detectives," Nancy explained. "Somebody stole our recipe for pink-strawberry lemonade and—"

"And you thought it was us?" Ben demanded as he slapped his pants legs silly.

"Not anymore!" Bess said. She pointed to the ingredients on Team Lollipop's table. "There are no strawberries on the table at all. And you're using sugar instead of—"

This time Bess clapped her own hand over

her mouth before she could say "honey."

Nancy studied the ingredients on Team Lollipop's table. Bess was right. No strawberries. No honey. Team Lollipop couldn't be making Hannah's recipe without those.

"Excuse me," Buggy said. "But can we start collecting my ants, please?"

Everyone turned to stare at Buggy.

"Your ants?" Gordon demanded. "Why on earth did you bring ants to a cooking show?"

"Because we're making a picnic basket," Buggy replied. "And what's a picnic without ants?"

"Give me a break!" Andrea groaned.

"Thanks a lot, Bug Boy!" Ben snapped at Buggy. "You just lost the contest for Team Lollipop."

"Well, that explains how the ants got in here," Ellen said. She looked straight at Nancy, Bess, and George. "Now why don't you girls tell me how *you* got in here?"

Before Nancy, Bess, or George could speak, Gordon pointed to the girls' hats.

"Does that say Louise Fayne Catering?" Gordon exclaimed. "I worked there right after cooking school."

"Louise is my mom," George said.

"And my aunt!" Bess added with a smile.

"Brilliant!" Gordon exclaimed. "I loved working for Louise Fayne!"

He turned to Ellen and said, "These girls meant no harm. It was that Buggy boy who brought those ants here."

"Sorry," Buggy said with a shrug. "I told my mom I'd rather be in the Bug Club."

A boy on Team Pepperoni raised his hand. "Are we ever going to start this contest?" he asked.

"Yeah," a girl on Team Popsicle said. "Our Quickie-Queso Cheese Dip is getting lumpy!"

Everyone listened as Ellen made an announcement. The contest would be taped the next morning when the studio was sure to be bug free.

"We're sorry that we caused trouble," Nancy

admitted. "We just have to find who stole our secret recipe."

She turned to Team Lollipop and said, "It's definitely not you guys."

Nancy dragged the picnic basket out from under the table. Before they could leave, Gordon invited all three girls to be on the show next summer. As Nancy, Bess, and George left the studio they could hardly believe it.

"Us on *Ready, Set, Cook!*?" Bess said excitedly. "I can't wait until next year!"

"What do you think we should make?" Nancy asked.

"Anything but lemonade!" George groaned.

Nancy, Bess, and George pulled off their hats and aprons and stuffed them into the picnic basket. It was the same place where Nancy had packed the Clue Book and pen.

"No ants inside the picnic basket." Nancy sighed with relief as she pulled out the Clue Book. "And Team Lollipop is innocent."

Nancy crossed Team Lollipop off the suspect list and said, "Now our suspects are Henderson 'Drippy' Murphy and Lily Ramos."

"Let's walk past Lily's lemonade stand on our way home," George said. "Maybe we'll find more clues."

"As long as we don't find any more ants!" Bess said with a shiver. "Ick!"

But when the girls got to Lily's yard, there were no kids or lemonade. Only a CLOSED sign on the table.

"I wonder where Lily is," Nancy said.

The sound of music suddenly filled the air. The girls glanced back to see Lily's cousin Carlos sitting on the front doorstep playing his recorder.

"Let's see what he knows," George whispered.

"Hi, Carlos," Nancy said as the girls walked over. "Where's Lily?"

Carlos stopped playing to look up. "Lily and her mom went to the supermarket," he said.

"To buy stuff for dinner?" Nancy asked.

"To buy stuff for her lemonade tomorrow," Carlos explained. "Her new and improved lemonade!"

"New and improved?" Nancy said. "How is it going to be new and improved?"

Carlos shrugged. He went back to playing his recorder until George yanked it out of his mouth.

"Hey—that's mine!" Carlos whined.

"You'll get it back," George said. "First tell us what makes Lily's lemonade so new and improved."

"How should I know?" Carlos said. "I'm just the entertainment around here."

"You've got to know something, Carlos!" Bess said. "Put on your thinking cap, please."

Carlos scrunched up his nose as he thought hard. His eyes suddenly lit up. "Lily said something about her new lemonade being her favorite color."

"Her favorite color?" Nancy said. "What is Lily's favorite color?"

"That's easy!" Carlos said with a smile. "It's pink!"

Chapter 6

SQUEEZE OR TEASE?

"Pink?" Nancy, Bess, and George exclaimed.

"Is that your favorite color too?" Carlos asked.

Nancy didn't answer Carlos's question because she had one of her own. "When are they getting back, Carlos?" she asked.

"They might stop for pizza on the way home," Carlos replied. "Lucky ducks."

Nancy, Bess, and George all frowned. If Lily and her mom were stopping for dinner, it would take them forever to get home.

"Okay, Carlos. Thanks." Nancy sighed.

"Can I have my recorder back now?" Carlos asked. He puffed his chest out proudly. "I can play 'The Wheels on the Bus'—backward!"

George tossed the recorder back to Carlos. As he played, the girls walked away from the house.

"Let's meet here tomorrow at ten o'clock," Nancy said. "So we can question Lily."

"What should we do until then?" Bess asked.

"Think *pink*!" Nancy said with a smile.

The girls walked home together. They waved good-bye as they each reached their houses one by one.

When Nancy got home, she found Hannah in the kitchen making dinner. She also found a pitcher of pink-strawberry lemonade on the counter!

"I made a batch for you," Hannah said with a smile. "Just in case you get tired of squeezing lemons!"

Nancy forced a smile. She had to tell Hannah they weren't selling lemonade tomorrow—at least not until they found out who stole the secret recipe.

"Um . . . we're not selling lemonade tomorrow, Hannah," Nancy said. She held up the Clue Book. "We're solving a new mystery. See?"

"A new mystery?" Hannah asked. "Is something missing?"

"Well . . . yes," Nancy said. "Something . . . top secret."

"Top secret?" Hannah chuckled. She nodded at her pitcher of lemonade. "I know all about top secret; that's for sure!"

"For sure!" Nancy squeaked.

Hannah turned back to the lettuce she was washing at the sink. Nancy placed the Clue Book on the kitchen table. She then turned sadly to the calendar on the wall.

How will we ever see Katy Sloan's concert now? Nancy thought. But as she gazed at the concert date, something wasn't right. The heart she had drawn on the calendar was *gone*!

Nancy's thoughts were interrupted by the voice of her dad calling, "I'm home!"

Mr. Drew walked into the kitchen. He smiled as he pulled off the tie he often wore for his job as a lawyer.

"Daddy, did you buy a new calendar?" Nancy asked as her dad kissed her on the cheek.

"A new calendar in the middle of the year?" Mr. Drew chuckled. "What made you think that?"

Nancy stared up at her dad. How could she tell him that the heart she had drawn on the calendar was gone? He would never believe her!

"Just wondering, Daddy," Nancy said quickly. She grabbed the Clue Book and pen, then hurried up to her room before dinner. Chip burst into her room too, hopping up onto Nancy's bed.

Sitting on the bed next to Chip, Nancy opened the Clue Book to a clean page. There she wrote:

> Clue: Lily has a new recipe for pink lemonade. Investigate tomorrow!

Nancy shut the book. Did Lily Ramos really take Hannah's top-secret recipe for pink-strawberry lemonade?

"If it really is Lily, Chip," Nancy told her dog. "I hope she's good at keeping secrets." She petted Chip and sighed. "At least better than *me*!"

"Wow!" Nancy said the next morning as the Clue Crew approached the Ramoses' yard. There were more kids at Lily's lemonade experience than ever before.

Lily was also in her yard next to her lemonade table. "Get your fresh lemonade here . . . made from scratch!" she was shouting. "Get your fresh pink-strawberry lemonade!"

"Pink-strawberry, huh?" Nancy said. "So that's her new and improved lemonade."

Nancy, Bess, and George walked over to Lily.

"You didn't have pink-strawberry lemonade yesterday, Lily," George said. "Why the switch?"

"Your pink-strawberry lemonade gave me an idea," Lily replied with a shrug.

"An idea or a whole recipe?" Bess asked.

"What's in it, Lily?" Nancy asked.

"I can't tell you," Lily said. "If you'll excuse

me, I have more lemonade to pour. Business is through the roof!"

As Lily began pouring her pink-strawberry lemonade, Bess pointed to the table.

"Look at the jar holding the money," Bess whispered. "It's shaped like a lemon—just like the jar Lickety-Split Lemonade comes in."

Nancy stared at the jar. The label was washed off but the jar was exactly the same as Lickety-Split's!

"You guys," Nancy whispered. "Do you think Lily is serving instant lemonade and telling everyone she made it?"

"I know how we can find out," George said.

George waved Nancy and Bess toward the Ramoses' trash cans against the side of the house. She then pointed to the blue recycling can and said, "If Lily made all that lemonade, she would have used a lot of jars!"

George pulled up the lid. The girls then stood on their toes and peered inside. Sure enough, inside the can was a big pile of—

"Lickety-Split Lemonade jars!" Bess gasped.

"Lily's lemonade isn't Hannah's recipe," Nancy decided. "It's just Lickety-Split!"

George was about to shut the lid when—

"Hey! What are you doing back here?" someone demanded.

The girls whirled around to see Lily. She had both hands on her hips, and she didn't look happy!

LICKETY-FIT

"Hi, Lily," Nancy blurted.

"Why were you snooping in our recycling can?" Lily demanded. "If you're looking for any of my old diaries you're out of luck!"

"We came to look for our pink-strawberry lemonade recipe," Nancy said. "It went missing yesterday."

"But you used Lickety-Split Lemonade," George said pointing to the recycling bins.

"Shh!" Lily cried. She lowered her voice.

"My customers think my lemonade is fresh—not a powder!"

"There's nothing wrong with Lickety-Split, Lily," Nancy said gently. "What's wrong is to tell everyone you made it from scratch when you didn't."

"I'm sure your aunt Maria wouldn't do that at her famous cafés," Bess added. "Would she?"

Lily began blinking hard. She then shook her head and said, "My aunt Maria does everything right. She's my hero!"

"So what are you going to do?" Nancy asked.

"I'm going to stop lying about my lemonade," Lily promised. "But I will keep selling Lickety-Split."

"Why?" George asked.

"Because I hate squeezing lemons, that's why!" Lily declared. "Did you ever squirt lemon juice in your eye by accident? Owie!"

Lily was about to return to her stand when Antonio Elefano from school walked over.

"Do you really allow pets here?" Antonio asked.

"Sure!" Lily said with a smile. "My lemonade experience is totally pet friendly."

"Cool!" Antonio said as he reached into his backpack. "Because I brought Stinky—my pet rat!"

Lily and Bess screamed as Antonio held up the squirming rat. When Stinky heard the screams, he jumped out of Antonio's hand onto the ground. When the other pets saw Stinky, they barked, meowed, and chased him through the yard!

"We'd better get out of here," Nancy told her friends. "Lickety-split!"

The girls left Lily's yard and headed toward Main Street. They had permission from their parents to buy frozen yogurt at their favorite store, Fro-Yo A-Go-Go.

"This place is the best," George said as she pulled the handle on the yogurt machine. "Where else can you fill your

own cup with any yogurt flavor you want?"

"And put on your own toppings!" Nancy added, squirting pistachio yogurt into her cup.

"Yogurt is yummy," Bess agreed. "But I'm sure going to miss Henderson's dad's ice-cream truck."

"Yeah." George sighed. "Mr. Drippy will probably be Mr. Squeezy now."

Nancy remembered Henderson stuffing something into his pocket as he left their lemonade stand.

"Henderson is the only suspect we have

left," Nancy said as they headed toward the topping counter. Suddenly a bunch of younger kids darted in front of them.

George recognized two of the boys, Mikey Pinsky and Victor Sung from her block.

"Mikey, Victor, hel-lo?" George called. "There's a line from the yogurt to the toppings!"

"We never got yogurt, smarty-pants," Mikey sneered. He pointed to the toppings. "Just this stuff."

"No yogurt?" Nancy asked with surprise.

Nancy, Bess, and George watched as the kids began loading their cups with gummy worms, licorice, tutti-frutti cereal, sprinkles, chocolate chips, raspberries, blueberries, pineapple chunks—the works!

"Hurry up, you guys," Victor told the others. "Henderson wants us back at his house in fifteen minutes!"

"Did you say Henderson?" Nancy asked the kids. "Are you talking about Henderson 'Drippy'—I mean—Murphy?"

The kids traded looks before Victor said, "We can't tell you. It's a secret."

"Does that secret have something to do with lemonade?" George demanded.

"How did you know?" a girl gasped.

Nancy, Bess, and George watched open-mouthed as the kids paid for their toppings and left.

"It *does* have something to do with lemonade," Nancy whispered. "We should follow them!"

"I know where Henderson lives," George agreed. "It's the house with the ice-cream cone–shaped mailbox!"

But Bess shook her head. "We're not going until I get my toppings," she insisted. "I can't eat fro-yo without blueberries and crispy coconut!"

"Okay," George said. "But after our fro-yo, we go-go straight to Henderson's!"

The girls poured on their toppings and ate their frozen yogurt. They then left the shop and quickly walked to Henderson's house.

Nancy, Bess, and George went to the front door. After they rang the doorbell several times, no one answered.

"Where is everybody?" Bess asked.

"Maybe the kids didn't go to Henderson's house," George said. "Maybe they just said that to trick us."

As they turned away from the door, Nancy noticed something way up in a nearby tree. . . .

"It's a tree house!" Nancy said, pointing. "Maybe Henderson and the kids are up there!"

They were about to head for the tree house when something round and yellow rolled out from under the garage door. It was a lemon!

Nancy looked at the lemon, then at the garage.

"Where there are lemons—there's lemonade," Nancy said, turning toward the garage. "Come on, Clue Crew. We're going in!"

Chapter 8

LEMON-RAID

The Clue Crew could hear voices inside the garage. When George rapped on the garage door, the chatter stopped.

"Is anybody in there?" George called.

"It depends," Henderson called back. "Who's there?"

"It's Nancy, Bess, and George," Nancy called. "We want to ask you something, Henderson."

"Not now," Henderson shouted. "We're busy in here."

"Too bad," George said through the door. "Because we have an awesome pizza with extra cheese that we want to share."

"Pizza?" excited voices cried. "Cool! Open the door, Henderson!"

The garage door slowly rose. Nancy, Bess, and George looked inside. There was no car, just Henderson and the kids from the yogurt shop. The kids were now wearing lab coats and goggles. They were standing behind a table filled with chemistry beakers!

"Wow!" Nancy exclaimed.

Also on the table were bowls filled with lemons and the toppings from the yogurt shop.

"Where's the pizza?" Victor asked.

"What pizza?" George said. She turned to Henderson and asked, "What's going on in here?"

Henderson shrugged as he mumbled, "Um . . . we're just whipping up a science experiment."

"It looks like you're whipping up lemonade!" Bess said.

"Okay!" Henderson sighed. "So you found my lemon lab."

"Lemon lab?" Nancy asked.

"We're trying to come up with thirty lemonade flavors," Henderson explained. "So my dad's lemonade truck will be just like an ice-cream truck!"

Henderson pointed to another table near the garage wall. On it were pitchers of lemonade in different colors.

“So far we made licorice lemonade, coconut lemonade, and pistachio lemonade!” Henderson said proudly.

“Don’t forget spinach lemonade!” a girl with goggles added. “It’s an acquired taste.”

“I think I get it,” Nancy said. “But why is your lemon lab such a big secret?”

“I want to surprise my dad!” Henderson replied.

The Clue Crew stepped back to whisper among themselves.

“One of those thirty flavors could be pink strawberry,” Nancy said. “Let’s look for our secret ingredients—and the missing recipe.”

“Good idea,” Bess whispered.

The Clue Crew strolled around the table studying fruit, candy, and vegetables. There was no honey, fizzy water, mint, strawberries, or recipe written on ladybug paper!

“Now what are you looking for?” Henderson asked.

“You were stuffing something in your pocket

when you left our lemonade stand," George explained. "What was it?"

"Something in my pocket?" Henderson gulped. "I don't know what you're talking about."

Henderson pointed to the open door and exclaimed, "Quit being nosy and get out of my lemon lab, Clue Crew!"

Mikey stood up with a lemon in each hand. "Or prepare for a squeeze attack!" he said with a grin.

The other kids stood up holding lemons too.

"Nancy, George, I can't get lemon juice on my new summer blouse!" Bess whispered. "Let's go . . . pleeeeeeease?"

Nancy, Bess, and George left the garage.

"They can't be making Hannah's secret recipe," Bess said as they walked away. "Not without strawberries, fizzy water, mint, or honey."

"But what was Henderson stuffing in his

pocket yesterday?" Nancy wondered. "I still want to know!"

As they approached Henderson's tree house, Nancy stopped. She looked up at the small house and smiled.

"Kids keep secret stuff in their tree houses all the time," Nancy said excitedly. "Maybe that's where Henderson put Hannah's secret recipe!"

The girls climbed the wooden ladder leading up to Henderson's tree house. One by one they stepped inside. . . .

"Holy cannoli!" George cried.

Henderson's tree house was filled with Katy Sloan pictures, CDs, fan magazines—even a Katy bobblehead!

Suddenly Nancy saw something tacked to a bulletin board. It was another picture of Katy Sloan, but this one was extra special. . . .

"You guys!" Nancy said, pointing to the bulletin board. "It's a picture of Katy Sloan—from our lemonade stand!"

PAGE PUZZLER

Nancy, Bess, and George studied the picture.

"It's ours, all right," Bess said. She pointed to the picture. "There's the date of the concert I wrote on it!"

"So that's what Henderson stuffed in his pocket." Nancy sighed. "Not Hannah's recipe—*our* picture of Katy!"

"Henderson still could have taken our recipe," George insisted. "He needs thirty whole flavors of lemonade!"

"Henderson never tasted our lemonade," Nancy said. "And there were no strawberries in the garage anywhere!"

"Here's why!" Bess called out.

Nancy and George turned to see Bess holding a red rubber bracelet in her hand.

"It's an allergy bracelet!" Bess said. "It has a cartoony strawberry face on it and it says 'Allergic to Strawberries'!"

"Henderson is allergic to strawberries?" George wondered out loud.

"That's why there were no strawberries in the garage," Nancy said. "And why Henderson didn't drink our lemonade!"

"So Henderson is clean," George decided. "Now can we leave before those lemon-squirting squirts find us here?"

Leaving their Katy Sloan picture on the bulletin board, the Clue Crew climbed down from the tree house.

"Thirty flavors of lemonade," Bess said as they left the Murphy yard. "Do you think they'll have chocolate-chip lemonade, too?"

Nancy's eyes grew wide. The words "chocolate chip" made her remember something important.

"I have to go home right away," Nancy said. "I promised my dad I'd walk Chocolate Chip."

"What about our case?" Bess asked.

"There's no case left," George said with a frown. "Henderson was our last suspect."

Nancy frowned too. With no more suspects or clues, how would they find out who took

Hannah's secret recipe? And how long could she keep the truth from Hannah?

Nancy hoped Hannah wouldn't ask about the lemonade stand when she got home. But she had no such luck.

"No lemonade again today?" Hannah asked. "How come?"

"Um . . . we couldn't sell lemonade today, Hannah," Nancy said, pretending to itch and scratch. "There were too many mosquitoes outside!"

Hannah shrugged, then walked back to the kitchen.

Nancy felt horrible as she hooked Chip's leash onto her collar. Why couldn't she just tell Hannah that someone took her top-secret recipe?

"Daddy?" Nancy asked as he walked by. "When is it a good time to give up on a detective case?"

"Give up?" Mr. Drew said. He smiled and

shook his head. "Sometimes the real answer to a mystery is the one you least expect. So keep at it."

Nancy never did like to give up. And neither did the Clue Crew.

"Okay, Daddy," Nancy said, grabbing the Clue Book and pen. "Then I'd better take these on our walk!"

Once outside Nancy walked Chip up the path to the sidewalk. While her puppy sniffed at the flowers, Nancy opened the Clue Book. But as she flipped through the last few pages she froze.

Something was weird. Terribly weird!

"Omigosh, Chip!" Nancy gasped. "I know I wrote in my Clue Book, but now it's . . . it's . . . empty!"

Clue Crew—and YOU!

Can you solve the mystery of the missing lemonade recipe? Write your answers on a sheet of paper. Or just turn the page to find out!

Nancy, Bess, and George came up with three suspects. Can you think of more? List your suspects.

Write the way you think Hannah's top-secret recipe disappeared.

What clues helped you solve this mystery?

Chapter 10

SURPRISE CUSTOMER

Nancy stared at each blank page. Everything had vanished like some magic trick!

"Our suspects and clues disappeared, Chip," Nancy said, tapping an empty page with the pen. "Just like the heart I drew on the kitchen calendar!"

Nancy stopped tapping to stare at the pen. It was the same pen she had used on the kitchen calendar. It was George's Presto Pen from her spy-girl kit!

That's when everything began to click. . . .

"I also used this pen to write Hannah's secret recipe!" Nancy said excitedly. "George may not know what the Presto Pen does, Chip. But I think I do!"

Nancy ran back into the house to phone her best friends. In a flash she and Bess were at George's door.

"I'll explain everything after I read the instructions for the Presto Pen," Nancy said. "Did you find them, George?"

George nodded and said, "The instructions were actually still inside the box."

But when the girls entered George's room, they froze. Sitting on the floor and scribbling all over the spy girl kit instructions was George's three-year-old brother, Scott!

"Scotty, no!" George said. "Give it back!"

Scotty put down his blue crayon. He pointed to the shiny charm bracelet circling Bess's wrist and said, "Give me that first. The *dragon* one!"

Bess whipped her hand back. "It's a unicorn!" she said. "And you can't have it, Scotty!"

Scott pouted and scrunched the instructions inside his fist. He was about to cry when—

"Give it to him, Bess, please!" Nancy said.

"Yeah, Bess!" George snapped. "You've got a million of those girly-girl things!"

Rolling her eyes, Bess snapped off the charm and handed it to Scotty. In turn,

Scotty handed George the instructions.

After unscrunching the instructions, George read about the Presto Pen out loud: "'The Presto Pen writes a supersecret message with ink that disappears within twenty-four hours. Now you see it. Now you don't!'"

"It's disappearing ink?" Bess exclaimed.

"Just as I thought!" Nancy said happily. "I used the Presto Pen to circle my calendar, write in the Clue Book, *and* write Hannah's secret recipe for pink-strawberry lemonade!"

"Wow, Nancy!" George said. "Are you saying—"

"Hannah's top-secret recipe was never stolen!" Nancy said excitedly. "It—poof—disappeared!"

"Poof!" Scotty laughed.

The Clue Crew traded big high fives. Hannah's top-secret recipe was out of sight but totally safe. They could ask Hannah to write it down again after they explained everything. And best of all . . .

"Our lemonade stand is back in business!" Nancy declared with a smile. "Katy Sloan tickets, here we come!"

Early the next day the Clue Crew sat behind their lemonade stand, happy to have solved another case. While Nancy stirred a pitcher of lemonade, a truck rolled by. It was the Mr. Drippy ice-cream truck!

"Guess what?" Henderson called from the truck. "My dad decided to keep his ice-cream truck after all. How awesome is that?"

"Awesome!" the girls called back.

They watched as the truck rolled away, playing the Mr. Drippy jingle. They were happy for Henderson, but not for themselves.

"We still haven't earned enough money for Katy Sloan tickets," Nancy said sadly. "And the concert is tomorrow."

"You guys," George said. "Maybe we should just forget about—"

"Katy Sloan!" Bess gasped.

Nancy and George followed Bess's gaze and gasped too. Stepping out of a sleek white car was the singer herself. It was Katy Sloan!

Nancy's heart pounded inside her chest as the star walked toward their lemonade stand. Katy Sloan smiled and said, "Hi."

"Y-y-you're Katy Sloan!" Nancy stammered.

"I'm in River Heights for my concert tomorrow," Katy said nicely. "I've been rehearsing all day, so I could use a cold cup of lemonade."

"We have lemonade!" George blurted.

"Pink-strawberry lemonade!" Nancy said.

"It's awesome!" Bess squeaked.

"Great!" Katy said. "One cup, please."

Nancy's hands shook as she poured Katy a cup of lemonade. The girls watched wide-eyed as their favorite singer drank. Did she like it?

"Oh, wow!" Katy said after drinking the last drop. "This is the best pink-strawberry lemonade I've ever tasted!"

"Would you like another cup?" Nancy asked.

"No, thank you," Katy said dropping a dollar into the jar. "But here's a little something extra."

The girls watched as Katy dropped three small red cards into the jar too. She gave a little wave and walked back to her car.

As the car drove off, Nancy pulled out the red cards. She looked at them and then let out a big shriek.

"Omigosh! Omigosh!" Nancy cried. "Three tickets to Katy's concert at the amusement park tomorrow!"

Nancy, Bess, and George couldn't stop

jumping and shrieking. They were going to the Katy Sloan concert!

"Nancy, George," Bess said as she stopped jumping. "We forgot to ask Katy Sloan for her autograph!"

"We can try tomorrow," George said.

"For sure!" Nancy said with a big smile. "But this time I'm bringing a *real* pen!"

A Star Witness

SPACE AND BEYOND

"That's it! That's them!" George Fayne cried as Mr. Drew pulled up outside the planetarium. She pointed out the car window. A group of people of all different ages was standing near the entrance. A woman with glasses and frizzy red hair held up a green flag with the letters RHAC written on it.

"That's the River Heights Astronomy Club?" Nancy Drew asked, looking at the group in front of them. There was a woman wearing a turtleneck (even though it was eighty degrees out), standing with a little girl a few years younger than Nancy, and a couple with white hair. It wasn't quite what she'd expected.

"Yup! Those are my friends Marty and Hilda," George said, hopping out of the car and pointing to the white-haired couple. "Hilda makes great banana bread. And that's Trina. She's the youngest member—only five. And her mom, Celia." George pointed at the woman in the turtleneck. "Thanks for the ride, Mr. Drew!"

Carson Drew smiled as he watched his daughter, Nancy, and her friends Bess Marvin and George climb the stairs to the entrance. "You girls have a great time today," he said. "I'll be back later to pick you up."

"Right after we see the Starship 5000!" George said.

"What's the Starship 5000?" Bess whispered to Nancy.

Nancy just shrugged. George and Bess were cousins, but they couldn't have been more different. George loved adventure. She went hiking on the weekends, was part of their town's astronomy club and their school's chess club, and was the first of their friends to try judo. She wore her brown hair short and only went to the mall when her mom made her go back-to-school shopping—or to buy another electronic gadget to add to her collection. Her cousin Bess liked spending nights curled up on the couch, watching old movies. She had wavy blond hair that went past her shoulders and had the perfect outfit for every occasion—whether it was a school dance or the state fair.

"How many meetings have you been to so far?" Bess asked as they walked toward the group.

"This will be my fourth," George said over her shoulder. "And the best—obviously. At most meetings we just eat donuts in the library and talk about stars and stuff. I haven't been to the planetarium since first grade!"

Nancy looked up at the giant white building in front of them. There was a dome on one side—that was where they held all the different space shows. She'd passed it so many times, but hadn't been inside since she was in first grade either. Now that George had joined the River Heights Astronomy Club, they finally had a reason to go back. George had been talking about the big trip for over two weeks now. The club was going to explore the museum and see a special show by a famous astronomer, Dr. Arnot, in the dome. George had invited Bess and Nancy along as her special guests.

"George! You made it!" The woman with the red hair checked something off her clipboard as the three girls climbed the stairs. "And you brought your friends. Delightful!"

The white-haired man named Marty smiled. "You must be Nancy and Bess!" he said, looking at them. "George has told us all about you."

Hilda peered over her tiny wire glasses. She pointed to Bess. "Aren't you two cousins?"

"Yup," George said.

"And you and Nancy have that club together," Marty said. "Solving mysteries."

"Something like that," Nancy said. She glanced

sideways at George and smiled. Nancy, Bess, and George had a club called the Clue Crew. They'd become good at helping people in River Heights figure out things they couldn't on their own. Sometimes someone's cell phone disappeared. Other times the Clue Crew found lost dogs. One time they'd helped Nancy's neighbor after her prize-winning roses were stolen. Nancy even had a special Clue Book she used to write down important details and suspects.

"George! You're here!" the little girl, Trina, called out. She ran over to George and gave her a big hug. She was dressed in black boots and a little green hat with a bow on it, and carried around a tiny pair of binoculars. Trina's mom smiled as George picked Trina up and spun her around.

"Wouldn't miss it!" George said. When she put Trina down, George turned to Nancy and Bess. "I taught Trina everything she knows about the Milky Way."

The red-haired woman patted Nancy on the back. She was older than Nancy's dad, and every inch of her skin was covered with freckles. "We're happy to have you girls. I'm Lois Oslo, the head of the astronomy club. As George might've told you, this is our sixth annual visit to the museum. Let's begin, shall we?"

She waved the green flag in the air as she turned inside. There were only seven astronomy club members besides Lois, so the flag didn't seem necessary, but Nancy followed along anyway.

When they stepped into the museum's front entrance, Nancy grabbed George's arm. "Wow! I'd forgotten how amazing it is."

They stood there, staring up at the fifty-foot ceiling. It was painted a deep blue with tiny glittering white stars. "I think I see the Big Dipper!" Bess said, pointing to the constellation that looked like a cooking pot with a big handle.

"You're correct," Marty said. Then he moved Bess's hand so she was pointing at a different cluster of stars in the sky. These looked like a smaller pot—one that you'd cook macaroni and cheese in. "And that's the Little Dipper."

"Yes, the entranceway is impressive," Lois said, pushing to the right, past a group of kids wearing Driftwood Day Camp T-shirts. "But not as impressive as the Hall of Planets."

They followed Lois into a room that had one long glass wall. Floating in front of the wall were each of the eight planets. Some of the planets had been hollowed out and were big enough to walk around in. People were climbing the stairs and wandering inside them, reading different information about Saturn or Jupiter.

Trina hovered next to her mom, pointing at each planet one by one. "My very easy method just speeds up names," she said slowly.

"I remember that!" Bess laughed. "Isn't that how we learned what order they go in?"

"That's right," Nancy said, going down the row. "Mercury, Venus, Earth . . ."

"Mars, Jupiter, Saturn, Uranus, and Neptune," Lois finished. "Very good, girls! Now let's take a half hour or so in here to look around, shall we?"

The group split apart, with Celia and Trina going straight for Jupiter. There was a window in the giant planet's side, right where its great red spot is. Nancy and Bess followed George to Earth. They climbed the stairs that wrapped around the planet and went inside the back. There were even seats so they could sit down.

A booming voice came out of the speakers. "Four and a half billion years ago, Earth was formed. It's known by many names: Terra . . . Gaia . . . the world. This, the third planet from the sun, is the only celestial body proven to accommodate life."

A screen on one of the walls showed videos of people from all different countries. One woman was weaving a basket and another was carrying pineapples on her back. There were scenes of panda bears and strange colorful insects, followed by underwater scenes of sharks and dolphins.

Nancy and her friends watched the entire video, then went on to Mars, reading a sign about the different rovers, or vehicles, that had landed on the planet's surface. They visited Jupiter and Saturn before noticing Lois and the rest of the group waiting by the exit. "We'll have more time at the end of the day!" Lois called. "I promise. But right now we should go see the north wing of the building, where there is a new asteroid exhibit."

Marty and Hilda waited for the girls to catch up. The group was almost out of the Hall of

Planets when they noticed an older man with wiry gray hair that stuck up in different directions. He wore a polka-dotted orange bow tie and had what looked like a mustard stain on his shirt collar. The man was standing in the hallway, talking loudly to a young woman who was wearing black-rimmed glasses and a red headband. She had on black Mary Jane shoes.

"Creepin' conundrums!" the man cried. "I can't believe that security guard nearly didn't let us into the museum. I forgot my ID today, so I spent twenty minutes trying to convince him I was who I said I was, and then I had to ask to speak to the planetarium director. I mean, really—you'd have thought I was trying to bring some wild hyenas in here! It was just a telescope!"

The young woman turned, noticing Lois and the rest of the group standing behind them. Lois smiled and waved at her. They must've known each other. "Dr. Arnot!" the young woman said. "This is the River Heights Astronomy Club! They're coming to your space show tonight.

Remember, I had told you about them?"

Dr. Arnot turned around, looking confused. It was clear he didn't remember.

Lois stuck out her hand. "Dr. Arnot!" she said. "I'm Lois Oslo. What an honor. I've watched your TV specials since I was a teenager. *Space and Beyond* is my favorite. Thank you so much for hosting us tonight; it's a special day for our club."

Dr. Arnot puffed up his chest and smiled. "Well, it is a pleasure to meet you too. I was just telling Kirsten here, I brought the Starship 5000—one of the most high-tech telescopes—on loan from an astronomer in Germany. Only one was ever made. The lens is more powerful than any other in the world. So you'll be getting a special treat tonight on the museum's roof. Now, if you'll excuse me, I have to find the director of the planetarium. We have a few things to discuss."

The man turned and disappeared down the hall. Kirsten smiled at the group. Nancy noticed she was sipping a grape soda. She'd been hiding it behind her when she was talking to Dr. Arnot.

Nancy remembered seeing a sign posted near the museum's entrance that said food and beverages were not allowed, so she figured that Kirsten probably didn't want Dr. Arnot to see her drinking in the museum. "I'm Kirsten Levy," she said, introducing herself. "Dr. Arnot's assistant. I'm so happy you're all here."

Lois beamed at the club's members. "I e-mailed Kirsten months back, and she was kind enough to arrange the special telescope viewing for us. Such a sweetheart!"

"So how long have you been working with Dr. Arnot?" Marty asked.

"For a year now," Kirsten said, and then she quickly finished the last of her soda. "He's very busy with travel and filming his TV show, so I help out when he's in town. I'm studying astronomy at River Heights Community College."

"Cool," Trina said. "So you want to be an astro . . . nomer?" She had trouble getting out the whole word.

"Yeah, I think so," Kirsten said. She pushed

her glasses up on her nose. "I love studying the stars. I'm actually part of a group project at school researching the Andromeda Galaxy. We're supposed to be presenting to the class tonight, but since I'm working here, my friend is going to cover for me."

"Oh, we'd hate to keep you from your presentation!" Hilda said.

Kirsten just shook her head. "No, this is one of my favorite parts of my job with Dr. Arnot. I love showing groups the night sky. He does an amazing planetarium show too. I think you'll really love it."

"We're going to explore the museum until the show tonight," George said. "What's your favorite thing here?"

"Have you seen the moon landing exhibit?" Kirsten asked.

George raised her eyebrows at Nancy and Bess. "A moon landing exhibit? That sounds awesome!"

Kirsten waved for the group to follow her. They went down a side hallway that led to a smaller room. The floor was grayish white with fake craters all over it. The walls were painted black with glittering stars. On one wall you could see Earth.

"It's just like we're on the moon," Bess remarked.

Nancy climbed on top of the replica of the moon rover. "Look!" she cried, picking up an astronaut's helmet. "They even have costumes."

Kirsten smiled. "I'm off to find Dr. Arnot. Enjoy the museum! We'll see you tonight!"

The rest of the group scattered. Some studied the

text on the wall beside the rover, which described the first time a human landed on the moon in 1969. Nancy and her friends put on the astronaut helmets. There were even puffy astronaut jackets that were all white with different metallic pieces on them. The girls put those on too.

"I can barely see out of this," Bess said with a giggle. She almost fell back over the side of the moon rover, but George grabbed her hand, keeping her steady.

Nancy climbed down off the rover, grabbing the flag that was there for a prop. She pretended to walk very slowly, like she was moving through water. She'd seen the footage of the first moon landing in science class. Buzz Aldrin had floated and bounced above the surface of the moon.

Then, with Marty and Hilda watching, she took her first step. Lois and two women standing nearby clapped. "One small step for man," Nancy said, some of astronaut Neil Armstrong's words echoing inside her helmet, "one giant leap for mankind!"

Chapter 2

A STAR-STUDDED SHOW

"What do you think?" Nancy asked, studying her friends' faces. "Does it look like us?"

Bess and George stared at the picture on the table in front of them. They'd found a man in the garden outside the Hall of Comets who was drawing caricatures of different kids. He'd even drawn the group of Driftwood Day Campers that Nancy had noticed earlier. When Bess, George, and Nancy sat down in front of him, he'd drawn them floating through space in astronaut suits.

They were holding hands with the Earth in the background.

"I think so," George said. "But our heads are three times bigger than our bodies in this drawing!"

"They're supposed to be that way," Bess said. "It's a caricature—a cartoon version of us."

"I hope my head never looks that big in real life," George muttered, shaking her head.

"Well, I think you all look amazing!" Marty said, leaning over to study the drawing. Nancy, Bess, and George were sitting with the rest of the astronomy club at the café, which overlooked the Hall of Comets. A giant model of Halley's Comet was right behind them.

Bess took a bite of the ice-cream sandwich on the plate in front of her and made a face. "Wait, what's wrong with this? It doesn't taste like ice cream. It's . . . dry!"

"It's astronaut ice cream," Hilda explained. "The kind they send to space. It's dehydrated, which means all the moisture has been taken out so you can eat it even in zero gravity."

"I love it!" Trina declared as she finished hers.

"It's yummy," Nancy agreed. She took another bite, letting the crispy chocolate cracker melt in her mouth before swallowing it down.

"All right, everyone!" Lois called, pushing her chair back from the table. "The big star show starts in five minutes. Is everyone ready to listen to world famous astronomer Dr. Arnot talk about space?"

"I sure am!" Celia said. Her black turtleneck even had a star pinned to the collar.

Nancy and the rest of the group followed Lois through the museum. Lois was still holding the green flag, waving it whenever the halls got too crowded. They climbed a flight of stairs and ended up right outside the giant dome. Kirsten was standing by the door.

"You made it!" she said with a smile. "Come in and have a seat wherever you'd like. Dr. Arnot will be here in a few minutes."

"Let's sit in the back," George suggested, moving down one of the auditorium's last rows. She plopped into one of the seats and leaned her head back, gazing at the dome above. "I remember this from when we were in first grade. Field trips here were the coolest."

"Didn't they make it rain in here somehow?" Bess asked, staring up at the ceiling.

"That's right!" Nancy said. "They used to have thunderstorms at the end of the show."

She was about to remind them about the field trip when Deirdre Shannon stood up and screamed as the water came down from the ceiling, but then the lights in the dome went out. Music blasted from a speaker on the wall. In the dim glow, Nancy could just make out Dr. Arnot walking in from the back of the room.

"So cool!" George said under her breath. The ceiling was now covered with stars.

"Thirteen point eight billion years ago there was a giant explosion called the Big Bang," Dr. Arnot began. "In that moment everything we know—all matter and energy—was born, including the sun, the moon, the stars, and Earth."

The picture on the ceiling changed, showing all the planets in the solar system, along with the sun. Dr. Arnot continued, describing how the planets were formed. Then he talked about the different types of life on Earth and how they all came from the same place.

Nancy and her friends kept their heads tilted back, staring up at the show on the ceiling. Dr. Arnot told them about the age of the dinosaurs, and the meteor that had crashed and caused their extinction. As he spoke, different images flashed across the ceiling. There was a giant Tyrannosaurus rex and a Stegosaurus. Then the pictures showed how certain animals may have evolved from the dinosaurs.

It had only been an hour, but Dr. Arnot had gone through nearly the whole history of the planet Earth. Then the dome changed so that it looked like the night sky, and Dr. Arnot pointed out different clusters of stars. There was Leo the lion, Pegasus, and Pisces the fish. The grand finale was the thunderstorm, just like Nancy remembered.

Thunder cracked and lightning streaked across the dome. Then, just like magic, water came down from the ceiling. A few rows in front of them, Trina held her hands up to the sky. "How do they do that, Mom?" she asked, laughing. "It's really raining!"

When it was finished, Nancy and her friends stood and clapped. "We haven't even gotten to the best part!" Dr. Arnot called out. The lights came on, and he led the group to one of the side doors. "Now we go up to the roof to do a little star gazing. This is where the Starship 5000 comes in handy. I own a few telescopes myself, but there's only one Starship 5000 in the entire world! It's such a special instrument." He gazed into the distance, and Nancy thought he looked like he might cry with joy.

"Dr. Arnot sure loves that telescope," she whispered to Bess as they all climbed the stairs.

"Can you blame him?" Bess asked. "It sounds totally cool!"

"I read all about the Starship 5000 in *Star*

Shine magazine," Lois said once they reached the top. "It's the best way to observe far-off galaxies, isn't it?"

"It's very precise," Dr. Arnot agreed. He stepped out onto the roof, the astronomy club following close behind him. "You can see Saturn and Jupiter up close and personal! A magnificent sight if you haven't seen them through a scope yet."

"I have, but I don't think George has," Lois said. "She's the group's newest member."

"We haven't either!" Marty said a little too loudly. He fiddled with his ear, adjusting his hearing aid.

Nancy and her friends walked over to the far corner of the roof, leaning over the short wall and staring out across River Heights. From up high they could see everything: the town hall, Main Street with a dozen shops and restaurants, and even the amusement park.

"Look! Our school!" Nancy said, pointing to a white building several blocks over.

Bess squinted at a house down the street. "Is that your—"

"Where is it?" Dr. Arnot yelped. He turned around, scanning the length of the roof. He checked behind Marty, as if the old man might be hiding something behind his back. "The telescope—it's gone!"

"Now, now, Dr. Arnot," Kirsten said. "Maybe someone brought it downstairs. It's probably just a misunderstanding."

Dr. Arnot's face turned pale. "Misunderstanding, fishunderstanding!" he cried, holding his head in his hands. "Call security—quick. Someone must've stolen it!"

A PLANET-SIZE PANIC

Three security guards ran onto the roof. Nancy and her friends stood there with the rest of the group, watching as the guards searched every inch of the place, looking under benches and by the emergency exit stairs.

"Creepin' conundrums! Kirsten and I moved it here just before the planetarium show. That couldn't have been more than an hour ago," Dr. Arnot said, looking at one of the guards. "I thought someone was watching it!"

A heavier man with a white mustache scratched his head. "I *was* guarding it. . . . I don't know what happened. I was standing right by the entrance to the roof," he said, staring at the ground. "I only let one group of people up while you were in the show."

"I checked on it once too," a redheaded guard added. "I was down near the Hall of Planets at the bottom of the stairs. When I looked twenty minutes ago, it was still here."

Dr. Arnot put his face in his hands. "It's not like it has legs. It couldn't have just gotten up and walked away."

"Now, calm down," the third security guard said. He was tall and thin, with spiky blond hair. Nancy noticed he was wearing a name tag that read STEVE. "It has to be here somewhere." He turned to the man with the mustache. "That group you let up here . . . who were they?"

The man shrugged. "They're a group from River Heights Greens Retirement Home that comes here every week. They are all women. A bit older."

"My grandma lives at River Heights Greens!" Trina jumped in. Her mom nodded.

"My friends Margie and Greta live there too," Hilda said, and sat down next to Marty on one of the benches.

Dr. Arnot started pacing the length of the roof. "Do you think they took it? It *is* quite valuable. Not to mention, beautiful," he added.

"I watched a bunch of them come down the stairs," the redheaded guard said, "and I didn't see anyone with a telescope."

"They were probably hiding it," Dr. Arnot said, wringing his hands. "I do hope it's all right."

Kirsten walked around the roof, checking under some of the benches, even though the guards had looked there already. She peered over the roof's short wall and then returned to the group. "It's like it completely vanished!"

"We'll start searching the rest of the museum," Steve said, ushering the other two to the exit. "It has to be somewhere. Don't worry, we'll find it."

But as soon as the guards went down the stairs,

the door falling shut behind them, Dr. Arnot shook his head. "This is terrible!"

Lois sat down beside him. "There are still a few hours before the museum closes," she said. "Hopefully they'll turn up something soon."

"Whoever took it might already be gone," Dr. Arnot said. "And that telescope is valuable! How can I go back to Igor and tell him I've lost it?"

Lois's eyes widened. "Igor Perchensky lent it to you? The famous German astronomer?"

That didn't seem to make Dr. Arnot feel better. When he looked up, his eyes were red. "Yes, Igor Perchensky!" he cried. "That's exactly who. It was his telescope. Tell me, how is anyone going to take me seriously after this? Everyone will know I lost it. I'll no longer be known as Dr. Arnot, world famous astronomer. I'll just be Dr. Guy-who-lost-the-very-important-and-special-telescope-and-should-never-be-trusted-ever-again."

"That doesn't have such a great ring to it, does it?" Bess whispered to Nancy.

Nancy looked at Dr. Arnot. His gray hair was a

mess, and his bow tie was crooked. It was hard not to feel bad for him.

"What do you think?" Bess hissed to Nancy and George.

"I think the Clue Crew has our next case," Nancy answered. She didn't look away from Dr. Arnot. He was telling Lois how he had finally become friends with Igor, an astronomer he'd admired for years. Now it would all be ruined.

"Let's get to it," Nancy said, already glancing around the roof for clues. She knew they didn't have much time. They had to find their suspect—whoever it was—fast. There were only three hours left before the museum closed and the telescope would be gone . . . forever!

Chapter 4

A PRIME SUSPECT

Nancy walked up to Dr. Arnot and pulled the Clue Book from her bag. She always kept it there in case she needed to write down clues or leads on unsolved cases. "Dr. Arnot," she said, "do you have any idea who would've done this?"

Dr. Arnot threw up his hands. "Anyone who wanted an expensive telescope," he said. "This one is worth more than five hundred thousand dollars."

Kirsten shook her head. "But not many people know that," she said. "Someone might have just taken it because they thought it looked cool."

"Well, I can't imagine it was anyone from River Heights Greens," Hilda spoke up with a frown. "They wouldn't do something like that."

Nancy wrote down "Motives" at the top of a page. It was just another word for why someone would commit a crime. She wrote everything she could think of underneath it.

Motives:
Wanted to sell the telescope
Wanted it for themselves
Thought it looked cool

"Was there anyone suspicious walking around today?" Bess asked. "Anyone who looked like they might be up to something?"

Dr. Arnot seemed to think for a

moment and then shook his head. "Not that I can remember."

George perked up. "What about that security guard? You were talking about him when we first saw you near the Hall of Planets. You'd said you'd gotten into an argument with him."

"Oh! Him!" Dr. Arnot said. "Yes, very rude fellow."

Kirsten clasped her hands together. "We were bringing the telescope in through the museum's side entrance," she said. "And he yelled at us. He was very annoyed that we didn't go through the front door."

Dr. Arnot puffed up his chest, impersonating the guard. "He said, 'Who do you think *you* are? What do you think *you're* doing?'"

"We explained to him we were just bringing it inside," Kirsten continued, "but he was really angry."

"I told him who I was," Dr. Arnot said, "and explained that I'd forgotten my ID. Then I asked to speak with the planetarium director, but that only made him angrier. He thought I was threatening him. I just wanted to bring the telescope indoors safely!"

"What did the guard do?" Bess twisted her thick blond hair into a ponytail as she spoke.

"His face got quite red—like a tomato!—and then he told me I'd be sorry," Dr. Arnot said.

George glanced sideways at Nancy. "Are you thinking what I'm thinking?" she whispered.

"Prime suspect," Nancy said, flipping the page of the Clue Book to write down the new information.

Suspects:
Security guard

"Can you tell us what he looked like?" Bess asked. "Do you remember his name?"

"He was a short fellow," Dr. Arnot said. "No more than five foot six. He was bald except for a tuft of blond hair in the center of his head. I can't remember his name, though. I don't think he had a name tag on."

Nancy wrote down the description in the Clue Book. "Do you remember anything else?"

Dr. Arnot sighed. "I think he had blue eyes and a little goatee on his chin."

"We shouldn't overlook other possible suspects," George said. "It might have been someone from River Heights Greens. They were up here last."

Hilda shook her head. "I don't think that's right. Why would any of those ladies want an expensive telescope? Plus, most of them are old and small. They would have trouble even carrying it down the stairs!"

Nancy wrote down "River Heights Greens," but she knew it was unlikely. Hilda was right. Most older women wouldn't be able to carry a telescope down the stairs without being noticed by security. Still, Nancy's father, who was a lawyer, had always told her she shouldn't judge a suspect by his or her looks.

“We have to look at anyone who might’ve been involved,” Bess said. “It helps to be thorough.”

“Someone might’ve wanted to steal it and sell it for money,” George added.

“But someone’s grandma?” Marty asked. “Do you really think that’s likely?”

Nancy glanced at her friends. She didn’t think it was likely. Not at all.

Nancy, Bess, and George moved away from the group to discuss the case. Bess looked down at the Clue Book in Nancy’s hand, pointing to the person listed at the top: security guard. “He’s the one with a real motive. If he was angry after his fight with Dr. Arnot, he may have taken the telescope as revenge.”

“But there must be two dozen security guards in the museum,” George said, “and we don’t have a name. What do you want to do, just wander around trying to find him?”

Nancy shrugged. “We could cover the place in an hour,” she said.

The girls looked at one another, knowing it

would be a risk. If they couldn't find the suspect, or if it took them a full hour to find him, that would be time they could've spent searching for clues. They weren't even sure he was the one who did it. They only had a hunch—a feeling about him.

"It's the only lead we have so far," Bess said. "So let's track him down and see what happens."

Nancy and George nodded in agreement. "You're right," Nancy said.

The girls said good-bye to Dr. Arnot and the rest of the group and then hurried down the stairs.

Chapter 5

BREAK ROOM BUST!

"Didn't we just pass that asteroid?" Bess asked with a groan, looking up at the giant black rock hanging from the ceiling. "I swear that's the third time we've seen it."

Nancy spun around, staring at the comets on the other end of the atrium. The café was still bustling with people, some eating the last of their astronaut ice cream. "I don't know," she said. "I thought we were going the right way, but now I'm not so sure."

They'd been searching the museum for almost thirty minutes, going through every hall and exhibit, looking for the guard. They hadn't found him anywhere. When they'd asked another guard if he'd seen anyone who fit the description, he'd gotten confused. "What do you mean he has a puff of blond hair in the center of his head?" he'd asked. "That's so odd!" Then the guard had chuckled and walked away.

Now they were near the café, which they'd

already passed three times. They couldn't figure out how to get into the other half of the museum.

"I thought it was that way." George pointed to an exit along the far wall. "Or did we come from over there?"

Nancy noticed a crowd on the other side of the atrium, beyond the café. It took her a moment to realize what it was. The artist who'd drawn them earlier was still there, making caricatures of more people.

"I have an idea!" Nancy said, starting toward him and motioning for Bess and George to follow. "We can have the caricature artist draw a picture of our suspect. That way we'll have something to show people when we're looking for him. It might help us find him faster."

Once they'd arrived, Nancy explained everything to the artist, whose name was Christo. She told him that he should draw a man who was five foot six, wore a security guard's uniform, and had a blond goatee. She even described his tuft of hair. Christo leaned over the drawing, working on the man's face. When Christo was finally done he spun the drawing around. "What do you think? Does this look like him?"

Bess stared at the picture of the man in the security uniform. "It definitely looks like the guard Dr. Arnot described. Maybe it will be enough to help us find him."

"Ahhhh," Christo said. "So you don't know him, but you're trying to find him. Well, if he works here, the break room might be a good place to start."

"The break room? Where's that?" George asked. She turned, scanning the café for anything they might have missed.

"It's actually right behind the café," Christo said, pointing to a door. "It's where all the museum employees hang out when we have fifteen minutes or so. I think I saw a few guards walking in there not too long ago."

Nancy raised an eyebrow. Now that they had the drawing, it would be easier to find the mysterious guard who'd threatened Dr. Arnot. All they had to do was ask around and show the picture. Surely someone knew him. "And he doesn't look familiar to you?"

Christo shook his head. "I haven't seen him before."

Bess walked toward the break room. "Thank you!" she called over her shoulder. "You've been a huge help."

Nancy and George followed her. Nancy held the drawing in her hands. When they got to a door that read EMPLOYEES ONLY, Bess didn't even knock. She just opened the door and slipped inside. Nancy and George shuffled in after her.

The room they stepped into had a large table with chairs around it, and a hallway off the back that looked like it led to a kitchen. Two women in security uniforms were talking over turkey sandwiches. "She told me the red highlights would be best with my skin tone," a woman with a short red bob was saying. She paused when she noticed the three girls standing by the door.

"Excuse us for interrupting, but we were hoping you could help us with something," Bess said.

Nancy held up the picture of the security guard. "Does this guard look familiar? We wanted to ask him some questions."

The red-haired woman, who had a name tag that said ALMA, laughed. "Well, what do you know? That is one funny picture of Bill. Look at how big his head is!"

The other woman, whose name tag said LOUISE, smiled. "Hey, Bill!" she called into the kitchen. "Some kids are looking for you!"

The man stepped into the room, scratching his bald head. Nancy could immediately smell his cologne—it was like a jar of oregano. "Me? Who's looking for me?"

Nancy rolled up the picture in her hands. "We were hoping to ask you a few questions," she said, "about where you were about an hour and a half ago."

The man's face went pale. "What do you mean?"

"A very expensive telescope disappeared from the roof of the museum," Bess explained. "The astronomer Dr. Arnot was borrowing it from a scientist in Germany. We have good reason to think someone stole it."

The man shook his head. Nancy noticed he wasn't looking at them when he spoke. That was always suspicious! "I didn't have anything to do with that," he said.

"Did you see Dr. Arnot bringing the telescope into the building earlier today?" George asked. "He told us you yelled at him."

"What does it matter?" the man said, pushing past them to the door. "I told you I had nothing to do with that telescope disappearing. Besides, I don't have to explain myself to a bunch of kids. Now if you'll excuse me, I have a job to do."

He stormed out of the room, letting the door

fall shut behind him. Nancy stared at Bess and George with her mouth open in surprise. "He wouldn't even look at us," she whispered.

"I know," Bess said. "He's definitely hiding something."

George and Nancy went to the door, peering into the café. Bill was weaving in and out of tables. He started down the Hall of Comets and disappeared into the east wing of the museum.

"Yeah," Nancy said. "But what?"

CAUGHT ON CAMERA

Alma followed the girls to the door, watching Bill go. "If I explain what's going on with him," Alma said, "you have to promise not to tell our boss."

George's eyes widened. "How can we promise that? If he took the telescope—"

"He didn't take the telescope," Alma interrupted. She walked into the kitchen of the break room, gesturing for the girls to follow her. Once they were there, she stared at the soda machine and finally pushed the top button. A can fell to the bottom with a clanking sound. She picked up the orange soda and opened it, taking a sip.

"If he didn't take it, does he know who did?" Nancy asked.

Alma glanced over the girls' shoulders at Louise, who had followed them into the kitchen. Louise was tall and had curly black hair.

"All right," Alma finally said, as if she was just deciding to tell them Bill's secret. "I don't know anything about that missing telescope, and I don't think Bill does either. But you girls were right—he *was* hiding something."

"He switched with someone for his last shift," Louise said. "We're not allowed to do that, but he wanted to work outside the café. He was supposed to be working in the Hall of Planets, though."

"Why did he need to switch?" George asked.

Alma laughed. "Well, you see, Bill has a little crush on Polly, one of the waitresses in the café. She only works on Saturdays, so one of his friends switched with him. He worked in the café and his friend went to the Hall of Planets. And Bill got to make googly eyes at Polly for two hours." She rolled her eyes.

"Two hours?" Nancy asked. She had pulled out the Clue Book and was writing down everything the guards said. "Which two hours? Are you sure he was there the entire time?"

Alma took another sip of her orange soda. "Hmm . . . must've been from four to six p.m. He just got off his shift."

George leaned over, looking at the Clue Book notes. "We went to the show from four to five," she told Nancy. "And Dr. Arnot had brought the telescope up to the roof just before that. So it must've been stolen in that hour window."

The other guard pushed through the kitchen to a door on the other side. She waved at the girls to follow her. "If you want to see for yourself, come on."

Nancy and her friends went into the room with Alma and Louise. There was another guard in there, sitting at a desk covered with computer

monitors. Each monitor showed a different part of the museum.

"Security cameras!" Bess said, pulling up a seat. "Why didn't you say something sooner? All we have to do is look at video of the roof and we'll know who took the telescope."

Alma sat down beside her. "There's only one problem. There is no security camera on the roof. What do you think, Paul? Can you pull up the four o'clock shift near the café?"

Alma looked to the guard on her other side, a gray-haired man with a mustache and glasses. He hit a few buttons on his keyboard and the main monitor showed the café. The time said 4:01 p.m.

"You're right," George said, pointing to the screen. "That's Bill, right there!"

Nancy narrowed her eyes, studying the black-and-white video. Sure enough, Bill was standing against a wall by the café. He kept looking and making silly faces at the waitress who was serving a table a few feet away.

"Can you speed it up so we can see the whole two-hour shift?" Alma asked.

"That would help," Nancy agreed. "Just so we can be one hundred percent certain he never left that spot."

Paul nodded. He hit a button on the keyboard to fast-forward the footage. Nancy could see Bill in the video. He shifted on his feet. At one point he checked his cell phone. But for the whole two hours he just stood there, giving visitors directions or waving to Polly.

"See?" Alma said when it was finally done. "I told you. He's not your suspect."

"He has an alibi," Nancy said. She'd learned that word while the Clue Crew had been solving other mysteries. An alibi was when someone was in another place at the time a crime happened. It proved that they weren't a suspect.

"If he's not our thief," Bess said, "then who is?"

Nancy flipped through the Clue Book, stopping at the page where she'd written down the list of suspects. There was only one other group of people they hadn't yet talked to. "The women from River Heights Greens."

"You really think they had something to do with the telescope going missing?" George asked.

"I don't know anymore," Nancy said. "But we should find them and see if they know anything—before it's too late. . . ."

Chapter 7

SNEAKY ON THE STAIRS

It took the girls almost twenty minutes to find the group of River Heights senior citizens. The women all had gray or white hair, and most were wearing Velcro-strapped shoes like Nancy's little cousins wore. They were huddled around the rover in the moon landing exhibit.

"This is silly," Bess said as she looked over at the group of women. Most of them had glasses hanging from chains around their necks. A few of them even walked with canes. They certainly didn't look like thieves. "There's no way one of them could've carried the telescope down the stairs."

George tucked her short brown hair behind her ears. "But maybe one of them saw something strange. You never know!"

The girls walked up to the group. Nancy pulled out the Clue Book, ready to write down everything they said. "Hi, there. We were hoping you could help us," she said. "We heard that you were on the roof of the museum between four and five p.m. today. There was a valuable telescope there that's now missing."

One of the women, a short lady wearing a pearl necklace, frowned and cupped her hand behind her ear. "What was that, dearie? You'll have to speak up!"

Nancy turned to Bess and George, who shrugged. So she repeated her words, only this time shouting them.

The lady looked confused. "A telescope? Why would we know anything about that? We sure didn't take it."

"MAYBE YOU SAW SOMETHING?" Bess asked in a loud voice. She clasped her hands together, hopeful. "DID ANYTHING SEEM ODD? DID YOU NOTICE ANYONE STRANGE ON THE ROOF WHILE YOU WERE THERE?"

"For gosh sakes, you don't have to scream!" a lady wearing a blue sweater set said in a grumpy voice. "Not all of us are deaf!" She scanned the group of women. "Where are Mildred and Susanna? They mentioned seeing something fishy on the roof."

Two women pushed forward. One was wearing glasses with dark lenses in them. The other was large and round and wore her hair in a long white braid. "That girl we saw," the one with the glasses said. "Is that what they're asking about?"

Nancy glanced sideways at George. What girl were they talking about? Was it possible they'd stumbled upon another suspect?

"What do you mean?" George asked. "You saw a girl on the roof?"

“The one with the telescope!” said the woman with the white braid. Nancy heard someone call her Mildred.

“We saw her take the telescope,” the other woman, Susanna, said. “She grabbed it and walked out with us. She marched right down the stairs and out the side door.”

Nancy couldn’t help but smile. They had finally found a clue! “What time did that happen? Do you remember what she looked like?”

"How old was she?" Bess chimed in.

Behind them, a group of Driftwood Day Camp kids ran onto the moon exhibit. A young girl with pigtails laughed as she climbed onto the rover.

Mildred pressed her fingers to the side of her head. "Well, I think she had freckles. And maybe brown hair?"

Susanna shook her head. "No, no, no. She had pimples on her cheeks. They weren't freckles. And she had black hair, definitely black. Wasn't she tall?"

Nancy held the pen above the Clue Book, but she didn't write anything down. Susanna was wearing glasses with thick, dark lenses. Was it possible her eyesight wasn't that good?

"She wasn't tall," Mildred said. "She was average height."

Nancy looked at Bess and George. There had to be a better approach.

Bess took charge. "Okay, what do you both agree on? Did you definitely see her with the telescope?"

"Yes," they said at the same time.

Mildred ran her fingers over her long white braid. "She went down the stairs with us and out a side door. I'm certain of that."

"Me too," Susanna said. "And she had a red scarf wrapped around her head, so it was hard to see her face."

"That's right," Mildred agreed.

Nancy scribbled down the things they had both agreed on.

Suspect:
A girl:
–Red scarf
–Went down the stairs and out a side door

George studied Nancy's notes. "And how old do you think she was?"

"Forty?" Mildred said, unsure.

"No, no—she was just a teenager," Susanna said.

They both stared at Nancy, waiting for her to write something down. Nancy didn't. This happened a lot with witnesses. They would both see the same thing, but they'd see it differently. They'd give two completely different descriptions of suspects, and Nancy would have to just look for what they agreed on.

"So she's anywhere from fourteen to forty years old," Nancy said. "She was wearing a red scarf on her head and she took the telescope down the stairs and out a side door."

"Which means it could already be gone," Bess said, frowning.

"I think that scarf was a disguise!" Mildred announced.

"Maybe," Nancy said. She looked down at the Clue Book, knowing they had less than two hours before the museum closed. They had to hope the mysterious girl was still here somewhere.

George scratched her head, the way she always did when she was stumped. "What next?" she asked.

"We could walk around," Bess said. "See if we run into the girl with the red scarf."

Nancy closed the Clue Book and tucked it into her bag. She smiled, knowing there was an easier way to find her. "I think I have a better idea!"

Chapter 8

A CLUE IN A CAN

Nancy knocked on the break room door. The café was emptier than it had been before. Polly, the girl Bill liked, was clearing off a few tables. A young couple was sitting by the wall, eating bowls of soup.

When the door swung open, Alma was standing there. She ran her fingers through her red hair. "You came back!" she said. "No luck with the senior citizens from River Heights Greens?"

"That's why we're here," Nancy said. "We

think you might have video of our suspect leaving the roof."

Alma shook her head. "I told you. There are no cameras on the roof."

Bess smiled. "Actually, we're more interested in the side exit at the bottom of the stairs. Is there a security camera there?"

Alma opened the door all the way, waving the girls inside. "There is. Let's see if Paul can find the footage. Do you know when it happened?"

The girls followed Alma through the break room kitchen and into the room with all the different monitors. Paul was still there. He'd opened a bag of potato chips and now crumbs were all over the table.

"It would have been between four and five o'clock," George said. "A woman came down the stairs with the group from River Heights Greens, and then she took the telescope out a side door."

Paul hit a few buttons on his keyboard and then pulled up a picture of a stairwell. Nancy could see a door at the bottom of it. He pointed to the screen. "These are the stairs that come down from the roof, and that's the door I think you're talking about."

He hit another button and the video sped up. The clock at the bottom showed the time. 4:00 p.m., 4:05 p.m., 4:10 p.m., 4:15 p.m., 4:16 p.m., 4:17 p.m. But it wasn't until 4:46 p.m. that the video showed anyone leaving the roof.

"There!" Bess said, pointing to a few women walking down the stairs. "That's them!"

Paul slowed down the video. It showed five of the women from River Heights Greens, walking down the stairs. They all held on to the railing. Right after they passed the camera, another group came down. Mildred and Susanna were with them. A girl in a red silk scarf was there too!

"That's her!" Nancy cried. "That's exactly who Mildred and Susanna described!"

Paul pressed the pause button, and Nancy, Bess, and George studied the picture. The girl was definitely in disguise, like Mildred had said. She was hunched forward, carrying something heavy in her arms. She was wearing black pants, but the red scarf was long, and its loose ends covered most of her shirt.

"Let's see what happens," Alma said. She reached over the keyboard and hit a button. The video continued.

Once the ladies from River Heights Greens had walked offscreen, the girl stood by the door. She looked around and then opened it a crack, pulling a can from her handbag and using it to prop open the door. Then she pulled something from under her shirt. It was the telescope! She ran outside, carrying it with her.

"Why is she going outside?" George asked. "And why did she need to keep the door open?"

"There," Nancy said, pointing at the screen. "That's why."

Just beyond the door they could see a car parked at the curb. Bess smiled. "She was bringing it to someone outside the museum!"

"Which means it's probably long gone," George said with a groan.

After less than thirty seconds, the girl came back inside. The red scarf was still covering her hair and part of her face, so they couldn't see any of her features. She spun around, looking over her shoulder, and ran up the stairs. Then she jogged off camera.

"She gave the telescope to someone," Bess said. "And then she came back inside. So she could still be here somewhere."

Nancy studied the screen. She pointed to the

can that the girl had used to keep the door open. "Can you please zoom in on that can, Paul?"

Paul hit a few buttons, zooming all the way in. They looked at the can the girl had taken out of her pocket. It had a bunch of grapes on the front of it.

"Hmm . . . ," George said. "So our suspect likes grape soda."

Bess plopped down in the chair beside Paul. He offered her some potato chips, and she took a handful, snacking as she stared at the screen. "Whoever she is, she must know that Dr. Arnot has realized the telescope is gone. She must know people are looking for it."

"What do you mean?" George asked, furrowing her eyebrows.

"She left the can there," Bess said. "If she's worried about getting caught, she might come back to get it. She wouldn't want to leave evidence behind."

Alma nodded. "That's a good point. Hopefully, the soda can is still there."

"We can have a stakeout," George added.

"We'll hide nearby, waiting for her to return to the scene of the crime. The museum closes in about an hour. It's our last chance."

Paul rewound the video to the moment where the girl went out the door. Nancy stared at her face, which was completely in shadow. Who was she? What did she want with an expensive telescope? And who was the person waiting in the car outside?

Nancy crossed her arms over her chest. Hopefully, they'd get answers before it was too late.

Chapter 9

COMET-HALL CHASE

Nancy leaned forward, looking out a small, circular window. She could just barely see the side door through which the girl had taken the telescope. The soda can was still there. She was starting to put the pieces of the puzzle together. It seemed like one person in particular took that telescope. And Nancy thought she knew who that person was. She didn't want to tell Bess and George until she was sure, though.

"Do you see her?" Bess asked. She was sitting

on a bench inside the giant model of Jupiter, looking out the window in the planet's side. The window was right where Jupiter's giant red spot was. They'd been hiding there for almost a half hour, waiting for the girl to come back.

"Not yet," George said.

On the wall inside the planet, a video played for the fourth time. "Jupiter is the fifth planet from the sun and the largest planet in the solar system," a voice blasted through the speakers. "It's a gas giant with a mass that's one-thousandth the size of our sun."

Nancy scanned the Hall of Planets. There weren't as many crowds as there had been just an hour before. A family with two small kids walked around the hall, but other than that it was empty.

"Come on," she whispered to herself as she stared at the stairwell. "Where are you?"

"Maybe she already left," George suggested as she sat down on the floor, pulling her knees to her chest.

But almost as soon as George said it, Nancy noticed a woman with a red scarf wrapped around her head come down the stairwell. The girl glanced behind her before going to the door and opening it a crack. She stared outside.

"She's here!" Nancy hissed. "It's her!"

George and Bess rushed up behind Nancy, gazing out the round window. "What is she doing?" Bess asked.

They watched the girl. She stood by the side door, peering out into the street. Every now and then she turned around, checking to make sure no one was coming down the stairs behind her.

"It's like she's waiting for someone!" Nancy turned to the entrance of the exhibit, knowing there was little time. "Come on. Now's our chance! We have to talk to her before she gets away."

Nancy ran down Jupiter's stairs and through the Hall of Planets, passing Mars and Venus. Bess and George followed close behind. When they were a few feet from the side door, the girl was turned so her back was facing them. They finally had found their suspect!

"Excuse us," Nancy said. "Can we talk to you for a minute?"

The woman straightened up. Nancy noticed she was wearing the same pants she wore in the security video. But it was only up close that Nancy saw her shiny black Mary Janes. They had a tiny apple embroidered on the side, by her toes. She'd seen the same shoes once before, earlier in the day. Any suspicions she'd had about who took the telescope were finally confirmed.

The girl paused for a moment, and then she knelt down and grabbed the soda can that propped the door open. Without saying another word, she darted past them and through the Hall of Planets.

"Hey! Wait!" Bess yelled after her.

But the girl kept going. Nancy and her friends ran through the Hall of Planets, across the museum, and into the Hall of Comets. The woman was pushing through a crowd of campers getting ready to leave. She didn't turn back—not even once.

"Hurry," George said as she picked up her pace. "We're losing her."

George was faster than Bess and Nancy, and she raced through the hall, passing the model of Halley's Comet high above. The girl with the red scarf turned down another hall that led to the museum's bathrooms. Because the museum was closing, both of the bathroom doors were locked. Their suspect was trapped!

When the girl with the red scarf realized this,

she turned around and sheepishly pulled the scarf away from her face.

"I thought so!" Nancy said. "You're the one who took Dr. Arnot's telescope!"

Bess and George stood there, frozen in shock. Could it really be?

Clue Crew—and YOU!

Can you solve the mystery of the stolen Starship 5000? Write your answers on a sheet of paper. Or just turn the page to find out!

Nancy, Bess, and George came up with three suspects. Can you think of more? Grab a sheet of paper and write down your suspects.

Who do you think took the Starship 5000? Write it down on a sheet of paper.

What clues helped you solve this mystery? Write them down on a piece of paper.

Chapter 10

A STARRY ENDING

The girl brushed her dark hair away from her face. Without the scarf, Nancy and her friends could see her glasses.

It was Kirsten Levy—Dr. Arnot's assistant!

Three important pieces of evidence had helped Nancy solve the mystery: Nancy remembered that when they first met Kirsten she'd been wearing the scarf as a headband. She'd also kept the can of grape soda she'd been drinking that morning, using it to prop open the door.

Then there were her black Mary Janes.

"I can explain," Kirsten said, her eyes filled with tears. "Please just give me a chance."

"Why would you, of all people, steal the Starship 5000?" Bess asked. "Dr. Arnot is your boss!"

Kirsten twisted the scarf around in her hands, clearly nervous. "I wasn't stealing it," she said. "That's the problem. This is all one big misunderstanding."

"What do you mean?" Nancy asked.

Kirsten let out a deep sigh. "Remember how I told you about the group project I was working on at school? Well, my partner realized the Starship 5000 would be the perfect telescope to use during the presentation. I knew Dr. Arnot would be too nervous to let me borrow it, so I decided to lend it to my friend during the hour that your group was in the planetarium show. Our school is only five minutes away, so I thought she could bring it right back."

"Right," George said, remembering what

Kirsten had told them when they'd first met her. "The Starship is the best telescope to view the Andromeda Galaxy. That's what your project was about."

Kirsten nodded. "That's right. So I lent the telescope to my friend, but her car broke down on the way back to the museum. I wasn't able to get the telescope here in time."

"So you lied about it?" George asked, crossing her arms.

Kirsten wiped her eyes. "I didn't mean to—at least not at first. It just happened. I was so scared Dr. Arnot would fire me. I was going to return it. I swear!"

"Where is it now?" Nancy asked.

Kirsten pointed behind them. "It's on its way. My friend is dropping it off any minute. That's why I was waiting by the side entrance. I'm meeting her there."

Nancy smiled at her friends. She knew Dr. Arnot wouldn't be happy that Kirsten had lied to him, but the telescope would be returned. Igor, the famous astronomer in Germany, would never even know it went missing. Wasn't that the most important thing?

Nancy turned back the way they came, waving for her friends to follow. "Let's go, then," she said. "There are only a few minutes before the museum closes. No matter what happened, Dr. Arnot will be very happy to know the Starship 5000 isn't gone forever."

Nancy and her friends stood at the bottom of the stairs, looking out the side door. It led to a street behind the museum. Kirsten sat on the bottom step, waiting for her friend.

After a few minutes a taxi pulled up. A girl with a brown ponytail stepped out, the Starship 5000 in her hands. Her skin glistened with sweat. "Kirsten!" she cried. "I'm so sorry! My car just stopped running, and I forgot my cell phone at school. I called you from the gas station I walked to."

Kirsten whispered something to her friend,

who then looked over Kirsten's shoulder at the girls. "Please—it's not Kirsten's fault," the girl said. "I was the one who wanted to use the telescope."

"I'm sure he'll just be happy to have it back," Bess said. She always seemed to feel a little bad for the suspects when they were caught.

"I'll explain it to him," Kirsten said sadly. She took the telescope from her friend and went back inside the museum, climbing the stairs to the roof. Her friend followed her, and Nancy, Bess, and George started up the steps after them. When they got to the roof the security guards were there, along with Lois and Dr. Arnot. The astronomer's face brightened when he saw the telescope. "Thank the heavens!" he cried. "You found it! Kirsten, you've saved the day! What happened? Where was it?"

Kirsten bit her lower lip. "Dr. Arnot," she began nervously. "I have to tell you something. . . ."

The man took the telescope from Kirsten's hands, holding it like a mother would hold a baby. He cradled it back and forth in his arms and petted it lovingly. Suddenly he whipped his head around and furrowed his bushy eyebrows. "What do you mean? What's wrong?"

Kirsten took a deep breath and started speaking. Her friend stood right beside her. She explained the entire story to Dr. Arnot, saying that she'd only meant to borrow the telescope for a half hour. She was going to bring it right back.

"I know I should have asked," Kirsten said. "And I shouldn't have lied when you found out it was missing. I'm so sorry that I made you so worried. I just didn't know what to do."

For the first time, Nancy noticed that Kirsten's hands were shaking. Dr. Arnot frowned, and then he finally spoke. "I'm very disappointed in you, Kirsten," he said. "And we'll have to discuss this later. But right now I'm just thankful that the telescope is back."

"It was always safe," Kirsten's friend said. "I took good care of it. If you want someone to blame, you should blame me—I asked Kirsten to take it!"

Dr. Arnot set the telescope down on the roof, adjusting it so it pointed at the sky. "Let's save the blame for some other time," he said. "There are only a few minutes before the museum is closed for the night, and I haven't seen a sky this clear and beautiful in a long time. What do you say? Should we all have a quick look at our celestial neighbors? Saturn and Venus are stunning through the scope."

That made Kirsten smile. "Thank you, Dr. Arnot," she said, dabbing her eyes.

"That would be lovely!" Lois clapped her hands

together like an excited child. Almost as soon as she said it, the other members of the astronomy club climbed the stairs to the roof, looking for them.

"You found it!" Celia cried. Marty and Hilda came up behind her. "We were wondering."

"Can I look too?" asked Trina. She stood on her tippy-toes, trying to see into the lens.

Nancy wrapped her arms around her friends, squeezing them into a tight hug as she looked up at the sky. It was a deep navy blue, with stars scattered across it like glitter. Dr. Arnot was right—it *was* beautiful.

"Good work, team," Nancy said. "We did it."

"Yes!" George said as Dr. Arnot showed Lois some stars through the telescope. "The Clue Crew cracks yet another case! And this one was out of this world!"

Big Top Flop

READY, SET, WHISTLE!

"The best part of spring is spring break!" George Fayne said. "And the second best part is that it begins *today*!"

"The best part of spring," Bess Marvin said, "is spring *clothes*!"

Eight-year-old Nancy Drew smiled as Bess twirled to show off her new outfit. Spring clothes and spring break were awesome. And there was one more thing about spring that she and her two best friends would totally agree on. . . .

"The best part of spring is the Bingle and Bumble Circus," Nancy declared, "which is why we're here today!"

Nancy, Bess, and George *did* agree on that. Each spring the circus came to River Heights Park. This year it came with something extra fun: a junior ringmaster contest by the big circus tent!

"Don't forget the rules!" Bess said. Her long blond ponytail bounced as she spoke. "The kid who blows a whistle the longest and loudest becomes junior ringmaster on opening day tomorrow."

"How can we forget, Bess?" George asked. "We've been practicing all week."

"I whistled so loud that my puppy, Chip, ran under my bed," Nancy said.

"That's nothing!" George said, her dark eyes wide. "I whistled so loud I broke one of my mom's catering glasses!"

"How was your whistling practice, Bess?" Nancy asked.

"I stopped when I found my baby sister sucking on my whistle," Bess said with a groan. "Gross!"

It was Friday after school, so the girls still had their backpacks. George pulled a plastic bag from hers. Inside were yellow candies shaped like lemons.

"Are those Super-Sour Suckers?" Bess asked, scrunching up her nose. "Eating those candies is like sucking lemons!"

"That's what makes them so cool!" George exclaimed. "They've got sour power!"

Nancy shook her head and said, "Sometimes I can't believe you're cousins. You two are as different as—"

"Sweet and sour?" George cut in. She was about to pop a candy into her mouth when—

"Excuse me," a boy said, "but where can a future junior ringmaster find cotton candy around here?"

Nancy, Bess, and George turned. Standing behind them was Miles Ling from the other third-grade class at school. Everyone knew that Miles wanted to be a ringmaster when he grew up. He even owned a ringmaster suit and tall black hat, which he wore today!

"You want to eat cotton candy before the contest?" Bess asked. "Won't it make your mouth too dry to whistle?"

"I don't want to *eat* the cotton candy," Miles said. "I want to stuff my ears with it!"

Nancy, Bess, and George stared at Miles.

"Stuff your ears with it?" Nancy asked slowly.

"That's how loud I whistle," Miles explained. "And when I whistle in the contest, you'll need some too!"

Nancy and her friends traded eye rolls. Miles may have been a good whistler, but he was also a very good bragger!

"We don't have any cotton candy," George said. "But you can have a Super-Sour Sucker."

George held out the bag. When Miles looked down at it his eyes popped wide open.

"N-no, thanks. . . . I've got to go," Miles

blurted. He then turned quickly and disappeared in the crowd.

"Do you think Miles was serious about stuffing cotton candy in his ears?" Bess asked.

"No," George said. "But he is serious about winning the Junior Ringmaster Contest."

"Well, so are we!" Nancy said, smiling. "In fact, let's make a deal. If one of us wins, we'll bring the other two to the circus on opening night."

"Sure, we will, Nancy," Bess agreed. "After all, we're a team even when we're not solving mysteries!"

Nancy and her friends loved solving mysteries more than anything. They even had their own detective club called the Clue Crew. Nancy owned a notebook where she wrote down all her clues and suspects. She called it her Clue Book, and she carried it wherever she went.

The girls turned to gaze at the big white circus tent with red stripes. Past the tent were rows of trailers.

"That's probably where the circus people and

animals stay," George pointed out. "Who are your favorites?"

Nancy smiled as she remembered the circus from last spring. "Oodles of Poodles are the best!" she said.

"I like Shirley the Seesaw Llama!" Bess said excitedly. "No one rides a seesaw like Shirley!"

"The Flying Fabuloso Family rocks!" George said. "Especially the trapeze twins, Fifi and Felix!"

"Fifi and Felix?" Bess said with a frown. "Those twins are trouble times two!"

"When they aren't on the trapeze," Nancy said, "they're playing tricks on other circus people!"

"Last year Fifi and Felix put some trick soap in Ringmaster Rex's trailer," Bess added. "His face was blue throughout the whole show!"

George shrugged and said, "The circus is all about tricks, right?"

Nancy was about to answer when the crowd began to cheer. She turned toward the tent just as Ringmaster Rex stepped out, waving his tall black hat!

"There he is!" Nancy said.

"And his face isn't blue!" Bess said with relief.

Mayor Strong and more circus people filed out of the tent. Fifi and Felix Fabuloso marched behind their parents.

"Will all kids please form a single line?" Mayor Strong asked. "Lulu the Clown is about to come around with a bag full of whistles."

The line formed lickety-split. The girls landed in the back with Miles right behind them.

"The best always goes last!" Miles bragged. "And that would be me!"

George groaned under her breath. "No wonder Miles is a good whistler," she whispered. "He's a total windbag!"

Lulu the Clown, wearing a gray wig, baggy dress, and striped stockings, walked down the line with her bag of whistles. One by one the kids reached inside and pulled out a whistle until—

"Eeeeeeeek!" a voice cried.

What happened? Nancy, Bess, and George stepped out of the line to see. A girl with curly blond hair had just pulled a giant squirmy spider from Lulu the Clown's bag. But when she threw it on the ground—it bounced!

"It's made out of rubber," the girl said, staring at the spider. "But it's still icky."

Mayor Strong raised an eyebrow and said, "Are you clowning around with these kids, Lulu?"

"I didn't put that spider in the bag," Lulu insisted. She pointed to Fifi and Felix snickering

to each other. "It's those Fabuloso Twins and their tricks!"

Nancy frowned. No surprise there!

"I thought the circus was supposed to be *inside* the tent!" Ringmaster Rex sighed. "Let's get on with the contest, shall we?"

Nancy, Bess, and George each pulled a whistle from Lulu's bag. So did Miles. When everyone had a whistle—

"Let the contest begin!" Ringmaster Rex boomed.

Nancy and her friends waited while other kids blew their whistles long and loud near the front of the tent. Finally it was their turns!

Nancy gave her whistle a long tweet but stopped when her nose began to tickle. Bess blew her whistle until she got the giggles. Then came George's turn and . . .

TWEEEEEEEEEEEEEEEEEEEEEEEE!

Everyone clapped their hands over their ears. George's whistle was so loud that even the horses in the circus tent whinnied!

George finally stopped to catch her breath. The crowd began to cheer. George was a whistling superstar!

"Way to go!" Nancy cried as George hurried back.

"You mean 'way to blow'!" George joked.

"Not bad," Miles told the girls as he walked to the front of the tent with his whistle. "Now prepare to be *blown* away."

"Don't worry, George," Bess said, handing her the bag of Super-Sour Suckers. George had asked Bess to hold them while she whistled. "You're the whistling champ so far!"

The girls looked on as Miles held his whistle between his thumb and pointer fingers. After clearing his throat he shouted, "Ladies and gentlemen and children of all ages! Introducing the junior ringmaster with the biggest, loudest whistle in the West . . . the East . . . the—"

"We don't have all day, kid," Ringmaster Rex said.

Miles stuck the whistle in his mouth. His chest

puffed out, then, *TWEEEEEEEEEEEEEEEEE!*

Nancy gulped. Miles really was an awesome whistler. But would he whistle longer and harder than George?

Miles's eyes darted around as he whistled. But when his eyes landed on George they popped wide open. Suddenly—*CLUNK*—the whistle dropped out of Miles's mouth. Miles's lips began to pucker, then his whole face!

The crowd laughed at Miles's funny faces. Nancy had a feeling it wasn't a joke. Especially when Miles stopped puckering and pointed angrily at George.

"It's all her fault!" Miles shouted. "She did it on purpose!"

Nancy turned to George, a Super-Sour Sucker lodged in her cheek.

Did *what*?

Chapter

NO SMILES FOR MILES

The crowd was still laughing as Miles stormed over to George. His hand trembled as he pointed to the bag of Super-Sour Suckers in George's hand.

"Just looking at those candies makes me pucker!" Miles complained. "That's why you ate them in front of me!"

"What?" Nancy said with disbelief.

"So I would lose the contest!" Miles said.

"How should I know Super-Sour Suckers

make you pucker?" George asked. "We're not even in the same class."

"Don't even say s-s-super-s-s-sour," Miles stammered, his face twitching again. Suddenly—

"Attention boys and girls!" Ringmaster Rex boomed. "The Bingle and Bumble Circus agrees that the winner of the Junior Ringmaster Contest is—"

"Georgia Fayne!" Mayor Strong chimed in.

"Yaaaaaay!!!" Nancy and Bess cheered.

"Did he have to say Georgia?" George said, cringing at her real name.

"And since Miles Ling made such funny faces," Mayor Strong went on. "The circus wants to make him junior clown tomorrow on opening day!"

Nancy smiled at Miles. She expected him to be smiling too. Instead his face glowed with rage.

"Clown?" Miles cried. "I didn't go to circus camp for three whole summers to be called clown!"

"Harsh," Lulu the Clown muttered.

Miles shot George one last glare before stomping off through the crowd.

George shook her head and said, "Remind me never to go trick-or-treating with Miles on Halloween. Did you ever see such a candy meltdown?"

"Don't worry, George," Bess said. "You didn't do anything wrong."

"You're going to be junior ringmaster tomorrow," Nancy added excitedly. "And we're going to the Bingle and Bumble Circus!"

The next day, Saturday, couldn't come fast enough for Nancy, Bess, and George. At one o'clock sharp the girls were driven straight to the park by Hannah Gruen.

Hannah was the Drews' housekeeper, but she was more like a mother to Nancy. She gave the best hugs, baked the best oatmeal cookies, and laughed at Nancy's riddles even if she had heard them dozens of times before.

As they walked onto the circus grounds,

Nancy gasped, "Look at all those people!"

"They're here to see the circus!" Bess said.

"And me!" George added a bit nervously.

It was too early for the show, but it was not too early to watch jugglers, acrobats, and clowns practicing right outside the tent.

Hannah was busy watching a man juggle plates when—*WOOF!* A snowy white poodle wearing a big collar charged toward the girls. Running after it was a boy of about nine years old.

"Gotcha!" the boy said, grabbing the dog.

Nancy smiled at the dog. "Omigosh—is that one of the Oodles of Poodles?" she asked.

The boy nodded, then introduced himself. “My name is Alberto,” he said. “I’m helping my parents train the poodles during my spring break.”

“That must be so cool,” George said.

“Most of the time it is,” Alberto said. “But Celeste here is hard to train. Today she refuses to wear her costume!”

Celeste gave a little yap before jumping out of Alberto’s arms.

“See what I mean?” Alberto groaned before running after Celeste.

“I don’t blame Celeste for not liking her costume,” Bess said. “That collar looked itchy!”

Hannah walked over with a woman at her side. The woman was dressed in a Bingle and Bumble T-shirt and khaki pants.

“Girls, meet Peggy Bingle!” Hannah said excitedly. “Her great-great-grandfather started the Bingle and Bumble Circus almost a hundred years ago!”

“I guess you can say I have sawdust in my blood,” Peggy said with a smile.

"That's got to hurt," George said.

"It's a figure of speech, dear," Peggy said. "How would you like a tour of the circus grounds before I show our junior ringmaster her very own trailer?"

"That would be George!" Bess said proudly.

Hannah was invited to have coffee in the circus performers' lounge while Nancy and her friends followed Peggy. They walked past the tent to what Peggy called the "Back Yard." She explained how the circus performers lived in trailers so they could travel from town to town. Some trailers were painted bright colors.

There were also a few smaller tents, like a polka-dotted tent called "Clown Alley," plus a big open tent that served food to the staff and performers. The girls were surprised to see everyone eating chicken, salad, and potatoes.

"I thought circus people only ate cotton candy and peanuts!" Bess admitted.

Peggy let the girls peek inside the wardrobe trailer, where bright sparkly costumes hung everywhere. A seamstress named Pearl sat at a sewing machine mending last-minute rips and tears.

"What's that loud rumbling noise?" Nancy asked as they walked away from the trailer.

"You mean that *growl*?" Peggy asked. The girls gasped as she pointed to cages and dens housing two tigers, horses—even a baby elephant!

"Do all the circus animals live here?" Nancy asked.

"All but Oodles of Poodles and Shirley the Seesaw Llama," Peggy explained. "They have trailers of their own."

"That's because Shirley's a star!" Bess said.

"Everybody is a star at Bingle and Bumble Circus!" Peggy said. She smiled at George. "Now let's show our junior ringmaster *her* trailer!"

Peggy led the girls to a shiny silver trailer. She opened the door and the girls filed inside.

The first thing Nancy saw was a ringmaster suit hanging from a rack. It had black pants and a red jacket with gold buttons. A shelf on top of the rack held a tall black hat just like Ringmaster Rex's!

"Is that mine?" George asked.

Peggy nodded and said, "Why don't you change into your suit right away? I'll knock on your door at show time."

Peggy left the trailer, and George ran straight to her costume. She was about to grab the jacket when—

"Wait!" Bess said. She pointed to a small sink in the corner. "Don't touch that beautiful costume until your *hands* are as clean as a whistle!"

"Since when are whistles clean?" George joked. "They're full of spit."

George did wash her hands, though. She then slipped on her ringmaster suit and hat.

"Ta-daaa!" George declared.

"Awesome!" Nancy said. "But something is missing."

"What?" George asked.

Nancy looked around the trailer until she spotted a long, silver object on the vanity table.

"That!" Nancy said, pointing to the table. "There's your whistle, Ringmaster George!"

Nancy, Bess, and George admired the supershiny whistle. It was engraved with George's name and the words JUNIOR RINGMASTER.

"They wrote George," George said with relief. "Not Georgia!"

"And this one can't be full of spit," Bess said with a smile. "It's brand-new!"

"Try it out, George," Nancy said excitedly.

George was about to give it a tweet when—*whoosh*—something slid under the door. It was a note written with green ink. Nancy picked it up and read it out loud: "'You're all invited to a cotton-candy party in the big circus tent. Come over right now!'"

"Cotton candy—yum!" Bess cheered.

"But Peggy wanted us to wait here," Nancy said.

"Maybe the note came from Peggy," George said, putting the whistle back on the table. "We should go to the party."

The girls left the tent, making sure to close

the door behind them. They rushed to the big tent and peered through the canvas opening. There was no party inside—only a few grown-up Fabulosos practicing a trapeze act. Their purple glittery leotards sparkled as they swung high above.

"No cotton-candy party in there," George said.

"Phooey," Bess said, disappointed.

Nancy didn't get it. "Then who sent that note?" she wondered out loud. Then—

"There you are!" Peggy called, rushing over. "The guests are about to enter the tent. George, we're almost ready for you."

"Okay!" George said. "I just have to go back to my trailer for my whistle."

"She'll be back in a flash, Ms. Bingle," Nancy promised. She, Bess, and George rushed back to the trailer.

Bess shivered as they walked inside. "Why is it so cold in here all of a sudden?" she said.

"Who cares?" George said, grabbing the

ringmaster whistle from the vanity table. "It's show time!"

The girls raced back to the big tent. George was whisked away by one of the show directors. An usher led Nancy and Bess inside the tent. Hannah was waiting in their special grandstand seats, right next to the circus ring!

"Watch out for swinging horse tails!" Hannah teased.

Nancy was so excited she could hardly breathe—especially when the lights flashed off and a spotlight began to swirl!

"Ladies, gentlemen, and children of all ages!" a man's voice boomed over the loudspeaker. "Please welcome Ringmaster Rex and our special guest, Junior Ringmaster George Fayne!"

"Yaaaaaay!" Nancy and Bess cheered louder than anyone as Ringmaster Rex and George entered the ring. When the cheering died down Rex and George stood in the spotlight.

"George?" Rex asked in a deep voice. "Do you have your whistle ready?"

"Sure do, Ringmaster Rex!" George replied.

"Then give a whistle, and let the circus begin!" Rex shouted.

Nancy and Bess squeezed hands as George put the whistle between her lips. Her chest puffed out and both shoulders rose. She leaned forward as she began to blow. There was just one problem: No sound came out!

"Where's the whistle?" Bess whispered.

"I don't know!" Nancy whispered back.

George's face seemed to redden as she blew even harder. Her arm flapped up and down as she kept trying to whistle. But no matter how hard George seemed to blow, there was no sound!

"Oh no!" Nancy groaned as she watched George. "Something is wrong!"

Chapter

FLEE-RING CIRCUS

"I can do it! Let me try again!" George cried as Peggy gently dragged her out of the ring. But before George could stick the whistle back in her mouth . . .

TWEEEEEEEEEEEEEEEEEEE!!! Ringmaster Rex blew his own whistle and shouted, "Let the circus begin!"

George was led away, just as a parade of circus performers marched into the ring. Any other time Nancy and Bess would have been happy to see them, but not this time.

"Hannah, I want to leave and find George," Nancy said.

"Me too," Bess agreed.

"But you girls will miss Oodles of Poodles," Hannah said. "And Shirley the Seesaw Llama."

Nancy could see her favorite poodles and Shirley in the parade. Also marching were Fifi and Felix Fabuloso in their own sparkly purple leotards.

"Shirley and the poodles aren't our best friends, Hannah," Nancy said. "George is."

"I'll save your seats," Hannah said with a smile. "But be back here in a half hour. No later."

Nancy glanced at her watch and promised to be back on time. As the horses pranced into the middle of the ring she and Bess stood up and walked out of the tent.

"There she is!" Bess cried.

Nancy looked to see where Bess was pointing. George was racing to her trailer. "George, wait!" she called.

"They gave me a broken whistle!" George shouted back as she kept running. "How could they do that to me?"

Once inside the trailer George slammed the whistle on the vanity table. Nancy tilted her head as she looked it over. Something about it was different.

"The whistle isn't as shiny as it was before," Nancy said.

"Maybe George smudged it with her fingerprints," Bess said while George slipped out of her ringmaster suit.

But when Nancy picked it up, she noticed something else. "George's name is gone!" she gasped. "So are the words 'junior ringmaster'!"

"You mean it's a different whistle?" Bess asked.

"Can't be," George said, still frowning. "It's broken. That's all."

Nancy shook her head and said, "I think the real ringmaster whistle was *switched* with a broken whistle."

George wrinkled her nose as she stared at

Nancy. "When did that happen?" she asked.

"Maybe when we left to look for the party," Nancy said. "Whoever slipped us the fake invitation probably wanted us to leave the trailer so they could do the switcheroo."

"But this is the circus—everybody is happy and nice!" Bess cried. "Who would do something like that?"

"I don't know, Bess," Nancy admitted. "But the Clue Crew can try to find out."

Nancy put the whistle back on the table. She reached into the pocket of her jacket and pulled out her Clue Book.

"You really do bring your Clue Book everywhere," George said, cracking a small smile. "Even to the circus!"

"And I'm glad I did!" Nancy said as she opened her book. A pen was tucked inside. She used it to write the words, "Who Switched Whistles?" Under that she wrote "Clues."

"The first clue was the invitation," Nancy said as she wrote, "written with green ink."

"There's another clue!" George said, pointing to patches of sandy dust on the floor. "Sawdust!"

"The circus ring is filled with sawdust," Bess said. "You must have gotten some on your shoes inside the tent."

"Ringmaster Rex and I walked in on a clear plastic runner," George said. She pointed down at her clean shoes. "My shoes never touched saw-dust!"

"Then someone from the circus ring tracked sawdust in here," Nancy decided. "Maybe a circus performer!"

"Or a sourpuss!" Bess said angrily.

Sour? The word gave Nancy another idea!

"Miles Ling was mad at George for sucking sour candies while he was trying to whistle in the contest," Nancy said.

"And Miles was asked to be a junior clown!" Bess added. "Which means he's probably here today!"

"We have no proof that a clown was in this trailer," George said. "Like footprints from giant shoes."

"No," Bess said with a smile, "but we do have *that*!"

Bess pointed under the vanity table. Nancy looked under the table and saw something red, small, and round. She picked it up, and it squeaked!

"It's a red rubber clown nose!" Nancy exclaimed.

"And it's small enough to belong to a kid!" George pointed out. "A kid like Miles."

"Does that mean I found a clue?" Bess asked.

"Yes!" Nancy said. "And now we're going to find our first suspect—Miles Ling!

Chapter

SAY SQUEEZE!

Nancy looked at her watch as the girls left the trailer. She remembered her promise to Hannah to be back at the tent in a half hour.

"We have ten minutes to find and question Miles," Nancy told her friends. "So we have to work fast."

"Miles could be anywhere here at the circus," Bess said. "Where do we look first?"

The girls spotted a jumble of arrow-shaped

signs pointing in all directions. Nancy read the signs out loud: "'Food Carts' . . . 'Blacksmith Shop' . . . 'Junior Clown Alley'—"

"That's it!" George said. "That must be where the Junior Clowns hang out."

The arrow-shaped sign pointed to a small white tent with colorful polka dots. The Clue Crew raced over to it. They peeked through the opening and looked around.

"No clowns in there," George said.

"No anybody," Bess added.

"Let's go in," Nancy suggested. "Maybe we can find clues that Miles was here."

The girls slipped inside the tent. It was filled with colorful clown props like giant baseball bats, tiny tricycles, and squirting soda bottles. A long table with mirrors held pots of gooey clown makeup and crazy wigs!

"Cool!" George said, pulling a rainbow-colored wig over her curly dark hair. "I've always wanted one of these!"

"And I've always wanted a pair of these!" Bess said, slipping into a pair of gigantic clown shoes.

George plopped a funny hat over Nancy's reddish blond hair. "Try this on for size, Nancy!" she said.

"There's no time to clown around, you guys!" Nancy said. "We have to look for clues that Miles was in here!"

Still wearing the clown gear, the Clue Crew searched for traces of Miles. But Bess found something else. . . .

"A clown car!" Bess cried out. "Let's see if we can all squeeze inside just like clowns do!"

Nancy turned. Bess was already squeezing inside a tiny car with big wheels. It was bright red and yellow.

"Come on, Nancy," George called as she crammed inside too. "Pile in!"

Nancy stared at the tiny clown car. She had always wondered what it was like to be inside one, so . . .

"Okay, but let's be quick," Nancy warned.

"Those Junior Clowns and Miles could be here any second!"

Squeezing inside the clown car was a tight fit for Nancy, Bess, and George—so tight that Bess wanted out!

"My foot is practically in my face!" Bess complained. "And I'm wearing giant shoes!"

"I don't like it either, Bess," Nancy said. "It's dark and stuffy in here."

"It's a plastic clown car, you guys!" George groaned. "Not a luxury stretch limo!"

Nancy was about to open the car door when she heard the sound of voices and loud thumping footsteps!

"Somebody's coming!" Nancy hissed.

"And they've got big feet!" George said quietly.

"Big feet mean clowns!" Bess whispered.

The Clue Crew sat silently inside the tiny car. They wanted to find Miles, but they didn't want the Junior Clowns to find them snooping inside their tent!

Nancy peered out the car's window. She could see about five Junior Clowns stepping inside.

"It's just our luck we had to be in the ring with Shirley the Spitting Llama!" a girl with a bright-red clown wig said.

"You mean Shirley the Seesaw Llama?" a boy asked.

"She's the spitting llama to me," the girl replied. "Clowns may rule but llamas drool!"

Nancy felt Bess tug her sleeve.

"I'm getting a cramp in my foot!" Bess whispered.

"Wiggle it!" Nancy whispered back.

The car shook slightly as Bess wiggled her foot with the giant clown shoe. Then—

HOOOOOOONNNNNNNNKKK!!!

Nancy, Bess, and George froze. Bess's giant clown foot had pressed the car horn!

"Hey," a clown said. "There's only one way to blow the horn and that's"—the girls gasped as the clown yanked the door open—"inside!"

Nancy and her friends spilled out of the tiny car. As they stood up they were surrounded by junior clowns!

"What were you doing in our car?" the girl with the red wig demanded.

"And what are you doing with our wig, hat, and shoes?" the boy wanted to know.

The clowns wore lots of makeup, red round noses, and giant plastic flowers on their jackets. Their names were stitched onto their jackets too, but not one of them was Miles.

"We just wanted to try on some fun clown things, that's all," Nancy explained.

"We're junior clowns too," Bess blurted. "Just like you guys."

Nancy heard George groan under her breath. Nancy had a feeling Bess's answer meant trouble.

"Oh yeah?" Mandy, the red-wig clown, said. "If you're junior clowns, then show us your best tricks."

"Tricks?" Nancy repeated.

"Every clown knows tricks," Spencer, a boy clown, said. "That is . . . if you really are junior clowns."

Nancy gulped. If she did know any tricks, she couldn't think of one now!

"Just go for it," George muttered. She picked up two juggling balls, but when she tried to juggle—*clunk, clunk*—dropped them on the ground!

Nancy turned a cartwheel. Bess hopped up and down on one giant foot.

Mandy pointed to the girls and shouted,

"Wannabes! I'll bet you never went to circus camp a day in your life!"

"Let's show them *our* favorite trick!" Spencer told the other clowns. "Shall we?"

The clowns formed a circle around the girls. Nancy gulped again. Now what?

"Ready? Aim?" Mandy shouted. "Gush!"

Nancy, Bess, and George shrieked. The flowers on the clown's jackets squirted water straight at them.

"Okay!" Nancy shouted as the water kept gushing. "We'll tell you why we're really here—just stoooooopppp!!!"

SLICK TRICK

The clowns finally stopped, but it was too late. Nancy, Bess, and George were dripping wet!

Nancy spit out a mouthful of water. "We're here to look for Miles Ling," she said. "Do any of you know him?"

While the clowns whispered to one another, Nancy studied their noses. They seemed different than the nose they found in the trailer.

"A couple of us know Miles from circus camp," a clown named Chloe said. "He used to get candy ringmaster whistles in his care packages."

"We know Miles wanted to be junior ringmaster," George said. "He became a junior clown at the whistle contest instead."

"Nuh-uh," Arlen said, shaking his head. "Something more awesome happened to Miles after the whistle contest."

"What happened?" Nancy asked.

"Miles went to Chicago with his parents," Arlen explained, "to film a commercial for Super-Sour Suckers."

"But Miles hates Super-Sour Suckers!" Bess said.

"A commercial director was at the contest," Arlen said. "He liked Miles's funny faces and asked him to pucker like that on TV."

"How do you know for sure?" Nancy asked.

"I was at the contest too," Arlen said. "I saw the whole thing!"

The Clue Crew traded looks. Was Arlen telling the truth about Miles? Or was he just clowning around?

Chloe interrupted the girls' thoughts as she

pointed to George. "Hey!" she said. "Aren't you the junior ringmaster who can't whistle?"

"My whistle couldn't whistle," George muttered.

"Bummer!" Mandy said. She held out a tall, colorful can. "Have some yummy peanut brittle to cheer up."

"I love peanut brittle!" Bess said, grabbing the can. But when she opened it three fake snakes sprang out of the can into the air!

"Very funny," Nancy told the clowns while Bess screamed.

"Sure, we're funny!" Arlen said with a grin. "We're clowns!"

The girls returned the clown gear before leaving Junior Clown Alley.

"I don't think Miles was at the circus today," Nancy said. "And that nose we found didn't belong to a junior clown, either."

"How do you know, Nancy?" Bess asked.

Nancy had the rubber nose in her jacket pocket. She pulled it out and placed it over her real nose.

"This nose is tiny," Nancy pointed out. "Even for a kid."

"There you are!" someone called.

Nancy turned to see Hannah walking toward them. She looked relieved but also a bit mad.

"I was looking all over for you," Hannah said.

"Sorry, Hannah," Nancy said. "We were busy doing something and forgot about the time."

Hannah looked the girls up and down. "You're

all soaking wet," she said. "How can you see the rest of the circus like that?"

"I think we've had enough of the circus today, Hannah." George sighed.

"And clowns," Bess added.

They were about to head for the car when George remembered something.

"I have to run back to my trailer," George said. "I left my jacket in there."

"Okay," Hannah said. "But this time—"

"We'll be right back," Nancy said. "Promise!"

Nancy, Bess, and George raced to the silver trailer. A blast of cold air hit them as they walked inside.

"No wonder it's so cold in here!" Bess said. She pointed to one of the windows in the trailer. It was half open.

Nancy stared up at the window. Did someone open it from outside?

"You guys," Nancy asked slowly, "do you think the whistle-switcher climbed in through the window?"

"The window is high," George said. "Why would someone climb through the window if the door wasn't locked?"

"So he or she wouldn't be seen going into the trailer?" Nancy wondered. She dragged a chair underneath the window and climbed up onto it.

"What are you doing, Nancy?" George asked.

"I want to see if there's a tree outside," Nancy explained. "Maybe the whistle-switcher climbed it to get through the window."

But when Nancy reached the window, she found something else. Scattered all over the windowsill was—

"Purple glitter!" Nancy gasped.

"So?" George asked.

"The Fabuloso Family was wearing purple glitter leotards!" Nancy said excitedly. "So were Fifi and Felix!"

"If anyone could climb way up there," George said, narrowing her eyes. "It's the Flying Fabulosos!"

"Fifi and Felix are always playing tricks too," Bess said.

Nancy hopped off the chair and smiled. Not only did she just discover a glittery clue, she discovered two new suspects!

"Maybe Fifi and Felix had a brand-new trick," Nancy said, clapping her hands to get rid of the purple glitter on them. "And this time it wasn't on the trapeze!"

TWIN SPIN

"Thanks for driving us to the park today, Daddy," Nancy said the next morning. "What will you do while we work on our case?"

"I'll read the Sunday paper here in the car," Mr. Drew said as he drove. "How would you girls like to work on the puzzles in the kids section?"

Nancy shook her head as she sat between Bess and George in the backseat.

"No, thanks, Daddy," Nancy said. "The only puzzle we want to solve right now is our mystery!"

Nancy had already told her dad about the case of the switched whistles.

"Do you have any suspects?" Mr. Drew asked.

"We're pretty sure Fifi and Felix Fabuloso did the switcheroo, Mr. Drew," George said.

"The proof is in the glitter!" Bess added.

Mr. Drew was a lawyer but often thought like a detective. He smiled at the girls in the rearview mirror and said, "Just be careful not to accuse Fifi and Felix right away."

"Why not, Daddy?" Nancy asked.

"Because sometimes even your proof needs proof," Mr. Drew replied.

Before Nancy could ask what he meant, Mr. Drew pulled up to the park.

"Thanks again, Daddy!" Nancy said as she and her friends filed out. "See you after we find Fifi and Felix!"

"Where do you think the twins are?" George asked as they walked away from the car.

"Maybe in their trailer getting ready for the next show," Nancy said.

"Or their next *trick*!" Bess said with a frown.

The Clue Crew reached the circus grounds. They were about to walk past the big tent toward the trailers when—

"Excuse me, girls," someone said.

Nancy and her friends turned. A guard stood behind them. The name on her shiny silver badge read FRAN.

"Kids aren't allowed on the circus grounds until a half hour before the show," Fran said.

Nancy knew they had to look for Fifi and Felix right away.

"George was the junior ringmaster yesterday,

and she forgot something in her trailer," Nancy blurted. "Can we go there and look for it, please?"

"It's her favorite pink hair barrette!" Bess added.

"Yuck, Bess!" George cried horrified. "Since when do I ever wear pink hair barrettes?"

Nancy was about to jump in when she noticed Fran smiling at George.

"So you're the one who couldn't whistle?" Fran asked.

"That was me," George muttered.

"Tough luck, kid," Fran said. She nodded toward the trailers in the distance. "You can go to your trailer and look for that pink barrette. Just don't stay long, okay?"

Nancy thanked Fran. As the girls rushed toward the trailers, George pulled the broken whistle from her pocket.

"Even the guard thinks I'm a whistling loser!" George complained. "Why won't this dumb thing work?"

George stuck the whistle in her mouth. Puffing

her cheeks, she tried to get a sound out of it. It was no use.

"It doesn't work, George," Nancy said.

"And you look like a blowfish!" Bess giggled.

George dropped the whistle back in her pocket. As the girls walked, they could hear dogs barking in the distance.

"We know Oodles of Poodles are here today," Nancy said with a smile. "But where are Fifi and Felix?"

"There!" Bess said excitedly.

Nancy looked to see where Bess was pointing. Coming out of the snack tent and eating bananas were the twins!

"Hey!" George shouted. "Fifi and Felix!"

The twins turned around. They were wearing light jackets over their purple leotards.

"What's up?" Felix called back.

"We want to know if you switched something in George's trailer yesterday," Nancy called.

The twins traded sly grins. Then Fifi said, "Maybe we did it."

"Maybe we didn't," Felix added and snickered.

Nancy frowned. The trapeze-twirling twins were tough nuts to crack. But before she could ask more questions, Fifi gave her brother a nudge.

"Whatever you do," Fifi whispered loud enough for the girls to hear, "don't let them see what's in your pocket!"

Pockets? The Clue Crew glanced down at the pockets on Felix's jacket. Both were lumpy with stuff. But what kind of stuff?

"I'll bet my whistle is in there!" George snapped. "The good whistle you switched with a dud!"

The twins spun on their heels and shot off!

"Don't let them get away!" Nancy cried.

The Clue Crew ran after Fifi and Felix. They were about to catch up when the twins tossed their banana peels in their path. Nancy, Bess, and George froze to a stop. Banana peels were slippery!

"They ran around the tent!" George shouted.

The girls jumped over the banana peels and raced around the tent. There they found the Fabuloso twins swinging from trapezes!

"Get down right now!" Nancy called. "And show us what's in your pockets!"

"Come and get us!" Fifi shouted as the two swung higher and faster.

"If you're not afraid of heights!" Felix laughed.

"Great," Nancy whispered. "We'll never be able to search Felix's pockets all the way up there!"

"Oh yeah?" George whispered with a grin. "Watch *this*!"

WASH AND CRY

What was George's plan? Nancy didn't have a clue as she and Bess followed George to the trapezes. But they were about to find out.

"Your swinging is awesome!" George shouted up to the twins. "But I bet you can't swing upside down!"

"Oh yeah?" Felix shouted back.

"Let's show them!" Fifi called to her brother. "On my count. Three . . . two . . . one . . . FLIP!"

In a flash the twins flipped upside down, still

hanging from their legs. As they swung back and forth—*CLATTER, CLATTER, CLUNK*—stuff from both twins' pockets spilled out all over the ground!

So that was George's plan!

"Ye-es!" Nancy cheered under her breath as they ran toward the stuff. "Let's look for the whistle!"

The girls scooped up two packs of bubblegum, a balled-up tissue that made Bess gag, a pen, and—

"A bar of soap?" Nancy said, picking it up. That was a weird thing to have in a pocket!

"But no whistle," George said sadly. "Anywhere."

Fifi and Felix were already on solid ground as they glared at the girls.

"You tricked us!" Fifi complained.

"Us?" George snorted. "If anyone knows about tricks it's you two."

"Where's George's whistle?" Nancy asked.

"What whistle?" Felix asked.

"George's ringmaster whistle that was switched

with a broken one!" Bess said. "As if you didn't know!"

"We found purple glitter on the windowsill of George's trailer," Nancy explained. "Just like the purple glitter on your leotards."

Fifi looked down at her leotard. "That's not purple," she said. "It's violet!"

"Give me a break," George muttered.

Suddenly the pen dropped out of Nancy's hands onto the ground.

"Nancy, that pen is green," Bess pointed. "Wasn't the party invitation written with green ink?"

George didn't mind getting dirty. She grabbed the pen and scribbled a squiggly line on her wrist . . . a green squiggly line!

"You wrote that party invitation to get us out of the trailer," George told the twins.

"So you could do the switcheroo!" Bess added.

"Okay, we did make a switch," Fifi said, "but it wasn't whistles."

"What was it?" Nancy demanded.

"Fifi! Felix!" a woman called.

Nancy turned to see Mrs. Fabuloso, wearing her own purple leotard.

"Come to the tent, kids," Mrs. Fabuloso called. "Uncle Alfonso is swinging by his teeth and wants you to watch!"

"In a minute, Mom!" Fifi called. She turned to the girls and said, "We'll take back our stuff now!"

Nancy and her friends handed Fifi and Felix everything they had picked up, including the green pen. The twins stuffed their pockets, and then they raced toward the big tent.

"They did say they switched something," Nancy said. "But they didn't say what."

"It still could have been the whistles!" George said. "And what kid carries a bar of soap around with him?"

Bess wrinkled her nose and said, "Speaking of soap, can I wash my hands? I touched that gross tissue!"

"There was a sink in George's trailer," Nancy suggested. "Let's see if it's still open."

The door to George's trailer was still unlocked. Nancy knocked three times. When no one answered she opened the door and they stepped inside.

"It's empty," George said. "I guess no one moved in after me."

"While Bess washes her hands, we can look for more clues," Nancy said.

Bess hurried to the sink and turned on the water. Nancy and George walked slowly around the trailer, looking up and down and all around.

"I'm pretty sure the twins snuck in here to switch whistles," Nancy admitted.

"Me too," George agreed. "What else is there to switch in here?"

Suddenly—

"Eeeek!!!" Bess screamed.

Nancy and George looked toward the sink. Bess was turning around slowly, horrified.

"Bess, what happened?" Nancy asked.

"My hands!" Bess cried. "They're . . . blue!"

SEE-REX!

Nancy and George stared at Bess's hands. They were blue—bright blue!

"How did that happen?" Nancy gasped.

"The soap on the sink is white!" George said, pointing to the sink.

"Then it must be trick soap!" Bess wailed.

"I washed in here yesterday," George said. "And I don't look like a Smurf!"

Nancy was still thinking about the word

"trick." It made her think of two people: Fifi and Felix Fabuloso!

"Fifi and Felix switched Ringmaster Rex's soap once," Nancy said. "And they said they switched something here."

"So they switched soap?" George asked.

"No wonder Felix had soap in his pocket," Bess said. "That was the good soap he switched with the trick kind."

"Okay," George agreed. "But while they were

here, those twins could have switched whistles, too!"

Nancy shook her head. "If they did, then your real whistle would have been in Felix's pocket," she said. "I think the twins are clean."

"But my hands aren't!" Bess cried. "How do I get this blue stuff off?"

"Let's ask Ringmaster Rex," Nancy said. "He can tell us how he got the blue off his hands when he was tricked."

Bess was careful not to touch anything as the girls left the trailer. Nancy took out her Clue Book. She stopped walking to cross the Fabuloso twins off her suspects list.

"We have no more suspects," Nancy said as she shut her book.

"Somebody in this circus switched my whistle!" George said. "We can't give up!"

As Nancy dropped her Clue Book in her pocket, she spotted a tall man with dark hair. It was Ringmaster Rex. He wasn't wearing his ring-master suit, but his twirly mustache twitched as he spoke on his phone. Rex didn't seem to see the girls as he turned away, still talking on the phone. . . .

"I told Mayor Strong that opening day was too important for a junior ringmaster!" Rex was saying in his usual booming voice.

The girls stopped in their tracks.

"Did he say junior ringmaster?" Nancy whispered.

"He's talking about me!" George hissed.

Nancy wanted to listen. She waved Bess and George behind a nearby tree. From there Ringmaster Rex's voice could be heard loud and clear.

"The junior ringmaster idea was a bad one," Rex went on, "but I'm glad I made the big switch!"

Nancy, Bess, and George exchanged wide-eyed stares. Did Ringmaster Rex say switch?

"The switch was worth it." Rex chuckled. "Who has the last laugh now? *This* guy!"

Ringmaster Rex ended the call. He pocketed his phone, and then he headed toward a nearby green-and-white trailer. Once he was inside, the girls darted out from behind the tree.

"Ringmaster Rex said he made a switch!" Bess said. "Could *he* have switched the whistles?"

"Rex said he didn't want a junior ringmaster," George said angrily. "He could have left me a broken whistle to make me look bad!"

"And just when we thought we had no more suspects," Nancy said, taking out her Clue Book. She wrote Ringmaster Rex's name on her suspect list.

"Let's go straight to Ringmaster Rex now!" George said, pointing to the trailer. "And demand to know where my whistle is!"

Nancy looked at Ringmaster Rex's trailer. Unlike George's, the windows were low.

"Let's peek through the window first," Nancy suggested. "Maybe we'll see the real whistle inside."

The girls scurried toward the trailer. When they peeked inside, the first thing they saw was Ringmaster Rex. He was standing in front of a mirror and peeling the mustache off his face!

"Omigosh!" Bess whispered. "Ringmaster Rex's famous mustache is fake!"

The girls watched as the ringmaster stuck his mustache on a piece of cardboard. The cardboard was lined with more twirly, swirly, and curly fake mustaches!

"Eenie, meenie, minie, mo," Ringmaster Rex said, pointing to each one. After choosing a big bushy mustache, he stuck it right on his face!

"Ringmaster Rex is tricking everybody with those fake mustaches!" George said, narrowing her eyes. "And I'll bet he tricked me by switching whistles!"

"We don't know for sure yet," Nancy said.

"I'm sure!" George said. "I want to knock on his door right now and—"

MWWWWAAAAAAAAAAA!!!

The girls froze.

"What was that?" Nancy murmured.

Turning slowly, the girls gulped. Standing behind them was Shirley the Seesaw Llama. But this time she wasn't riding a seesaw with her owners.

This time she was *spitting*!

ALL EARS

MWWWWAAAAAAAAAA!!! Shirley groaned again.

Nancy, Bess, and George wanted to run, but Shirley was backing them against the trailer.

"Gob rockets!" George shouted as Shirley fired spit in the girls' direction. "Duck!"

The Clue Crew did a good job dodging Shirley's spit until Ringmaster Rex ran out of his trailer.

"What on earth is going on out here?" Rex demanded.

"Why don't you ask Shirley the Seesaw Llama?" George said. "She's the one who attacked us!"

The ringmaster looked at Shirley. His new mustache wiggled as he flashed a smile.

"You mean Shirley the *guard* llama," Rex replied.

"Guard llama?" Nancy repeated.

"Llamas are often used to guard sheep from coyotes," Rex explained. "Shirley was a guard llama before she joined the circus."

Ringmaster Rex reached out to gently pat Shirley. "I guess now she guards our trailers," he said.

When Shirley calmed down, Ringmaster Rex turned to George.

"Weren't you the junior ringmaster yesterday?" Rex asked. "The one with a whistling problem?"

"It wasn't George's fault, Ringmaster Rex," Nancy said. "Her whistle was switched with a broken one."

"We think the one who did the switcheroo," George said, folding her arms across her chest, "is you!"

"Me?" Ringmaster Rex exclaimed. "Why, I did nothing of the kind!"

"We overheard you talking on the phone," Nancy said. "You said something about making a switch."

"What else could it be but whistles?" Bess asked.

"How about . . . trailers?" Rex asked slowly.

"Trailers?" Nancy and her friends said together.

"Peggy asked me to switch trailers with the junior ringmaster," Rex explained. "My trailer was bigger and closer to the big tent."

"So why are you glad you made the switch?" Nancy asked.

"Because this one has Wi-Fi!" Rex said, pointing to the green-and-white trailer. "How cool is that?"

Ringmaster Rex tugged Shirley by her collar and said, "I'll bring Miss Shirley back to her owners now."

Nancy, Bess, and George watched as Ringmaster Rex gently led Shirley toward the tent.

"How do we know he told us the truth about switching trailers?" George asked.

"If Ringmaster Rex fooled us with his fake mustaches," Bess said, "he could be fooling us with a fake story!"

But the fake mustaches gave Nancy an idea.

"I know how we can find out if Ringmaster Rex is telling the truth," Nancy said. "We can give him an honesty test!"

The girls waited until the ringmaster returned.

"Ringmaster Rex?" Nancy asked bravely. "Is your mustache real . . . or fake?"

Ringmaster Rex's eyes widened. He glanced

both ways, and then he leaned over and whispered, "None of my mustaches are real. They're the press-on kind."

"No way!" Nancy said, pretending to be surprised.

"It's true," Rex admitted. "Now, can you girls promise to keep my mustaches a secret?"

"If you tell us another secret," Bess said. She raised her hands. "How do you get trick soap off?"

"Regular soap and water," Rex said with a grin. "Good luck!"

As the ringmaster walked into his trailer, Nancy crossed his name off her suspect list.

"If Ringmaster Rex was honest about his mustache," Nancy said, "he must be honest about switching trailers, not whistles."

"But now we have no suspects again." Bess frowned.

"What about Miles?" George said. "He didn't have to be a junior clown to be at the circus yesterday."

"How do we know Miles is really in Chicago,

filming a commercial for Super-Sour Suckers?" Bess said.

Nancy was about to give Miles a thought when—

"Girls?" someone called. "What are you still doing here?"

Nancy, Bess, and George whirled around. Walking toward them was the guard Fran.

"We were just leaving!" Nancy said.

"Did you find what you were looking for?" Fran asked.

Nancy thought about George's whistle and shook her head. "No," she replied, "but we're not going to give up!"

Bess didn't want to mess up Mr. Drew's car with her blue hands, so the Clue Crew walked back to Nancy's house. The girls all had the same rules: They could walk anywhere as long as it was fewer than five blocks away and they were together.

"We can work on our case while we eat lunch,"

Nancy said. "If we're lucky, Hannah will have lots of her yummy tuna salad."

"And real soap," Bess said, frowning down at her hands.

When the girls reached the Drew house, Bess went straight to the bathroom to wash her hands. Then they waited in Nancy's room while Hannah prepared lunch.

"I think I'll check my e-mails," George said as she sat at Nancy's computer and went online.

"Shouldn't we be working on the case?" Bess asked.

"We *are* working on the case," George said, staring at the computer screen. "I just got an e-mail from Miles!"

"Miles?" Nancy asked. She and Bess peered over George's shoulders as she read Miles's e-mail out loud: "'You may have won that dumb whistling contest, Fayne, but look what I'm getting to do. Jealous much?'"

Miles had attached a video. George clicked on it. The video showed Miles on a TV set!

"Super-Sour Suckers mean extreeeeme puckers!" Miles said into a camera. He popped a candy into his mouth. Soon his lips began to pucker—then his whole face!

"That's the same face Miles made at the whistle-blowing contest!" Bess said.

"Look!" Nancy said. She pointed to the date in the corner of the video. "That's the day George's whistle went missing."

"But how do we know he's filming the commercial in Chicago?" Bess asked.

"The cameraman is wearing a Cubs jersey," George pointed out. "That's a Chicago baseball team."

"So Miles wasn't around to switch whistles," Nancy decided, "instead he's a TV star."

"And I'm still a junior ringmaster with a busted whistle." George sighed. She pulled her broken whistle out and stuck it in her mouth.

"It's no use, George," Nancy said. "You're never going to get a sound out of that thing."

Woof! Woof! Woof!

Nancy's puppy, Chocolate Chip, suddenly came running in. George dropped the whistle as Chip jumped up on her, wagging her tail and still barking.

"You would think Chip heard my whistle!" George chuckled.

Nancy was about to call her dog, but then something suddenly clicked.

"You guys!" Nancy said. "Maybe Chip did!"

"Did what?" Bess asked.

Nancy smiled and said, "Maybe Chip did hear the whistle!"

Clue Crew—and YOU!

Can you solve the mystery of the circus whistle-switcher? Try thinking like the Clue Crew, or turn the page to find out!

1. The Clue Crew ruled out all their suspects. Can you think of others? Write them down on a piece of paper!

2. Nancy thinks that Chocolate Chip might have heard George's whistle. How would that be possible? Write down some reasons on a sheet of paper.

3. The Clue Crew discovered glitter and a red rubber clown nose in George's trailer. What other clues would you have looked for? Write your possible clues on a sheet of paper!

BARK IN THE PARK

"I don't get it, Nancy," Bess said. "How could Chip hear the whistle when we didn't?"

"It might be a whistle that only dogs can hear," Nancy explained. "Dogs can hear things that humans can't."

"I've heard of dog whistles before!" George said. "Do you think this whistle is one?"

"Remember how Oodles of Poodles barked today at the circus?" Bess asked. "When you tried to blow your whistle, George?"

George nodded and said, "We didn't hear it, but the poodles did."

Nancy gave her puppy a big hug to say thanks. She had given them the best clue ever!

"I don't think the good whistle was switched with a broken whistle," Nancy said. "I think it was switched with a *dog* whistle!"

"But what if only Chip can hear it?" Bess asked. "We should test the whistle out on other dogs."

"Yes, and I know just the place to do it," Nancy said. "The dog run!"

Nancy, Bess, and George ate tuna sandwiches and then hurried to the dog run inside River Heights Park. From there they could see the circus tent.

"We've come to the right place," George said as they filed through the gate. "Look at all those dogs!"

Nancy saw dogs of all sizes,

scampering about with their owners. Would they stop playing if they heard the whistle? There was only one way to find out. . . .

"Okay, George," Nancy said. "Ready? Set? Blow!"

George stuck the whistle in her mouth and blew. Nancy didn't hear a thing, but that didn't matter. Could the dogs?

"Look!" Bess said, pointing to the dogs. One dropped his Frisbee as his ears perked up. Another was running toward George. Soon more dogs were charging toward George!

Woof, woof! Arf, arf!

"Testing complete!" George chuckled when she was surrounded by dogs. "My whistle *was* switched with a dog whistle!"

"There's only one dog act in the circus—Oodles of Poodles," Nancy said. "Maybe the whistle was Alberto's!"

"How do we know Alberto was in my trailer?" George asked. "The clown nose we found has nothing to do with dogs!"

Nancy watched as owners came to retrieve their dogs. One poodle reminded her of Alberto's dog, Celeste. That reminded her of something else. . . .

"Alberto's poodle wore a big collar just like a clown's," Nancy said. "Maybe part of her costume was a rubber clown *nose*!"

"Ewwww!" Bess exclaimed. "That means you tried on a dog's rubber nose, Nancy!"

Nancy didn't care. She just cared about putting the puzzle pieces together.

"I think the clown in George's trailer was funny and furry," Nancy declared. "I think the clown was a dog!"

The Clue Crew left the dog park and raced straight to the circus grounds. The show would start in a half-hour.

"How are we going to find Alberto?" Nancy asked.

"Here's how!" George said. She pulled out the whistle and blew. Soon—

Woof, woof, woof!

In a flash the Oodles of Poodles came running with Alberto right behind. The dogs were dressed up as clowns again. The only dog without a red rubber nose was Celeste!

"How did you get my dogs to run over?" Alberto asked.

"Easy!" George said, holding up the whistle. "Look familiar?"

Alberto's eyes popped open when he saw the whistle. He shook his head hard and stammered, "I—I—I don't remember!"

"Does this help your memory?" Nancy asked as she pulled the red rubber nose from her pocket.

When Alberto saw the nose, he gulped. He then took a deep breath and said, "That's my dog whistle. I left it in George's trailer."

Nancy's heart did a triple flip. Alberto had just confessed!

"The door was wide open," Alberto went on. "Celeste ran inside and under the table."

"But I closed the door when we left," George said.

"Maybe Fifi and Felix left the door open," Nancy figured, "when they left the trailer."

"I crawled under the table to get Celeste," Alberto continued, "but first I put my dog whistle on the table."

Alberto shrugged and said, "I grabbed Celeste, then my whistle before I left. I guess I grabbed the ringmaster whistle by mistake."

"And I got the dog whistle you left behind," George said glumly. "Thanks a lot, poodle boy."

"It was an accident!" Alberto said. "By the

time I knew I had the wrong whistle, you were already in the tent."

"Why didn't you tell us, Alberto?" Nancy asked.

"I felt too bad," Alberto admitted. "Because of me George's junior ringmaster moment was ruined."

Alberto reached into his pocket and pulled out a shiny silver whistle. It was so shiny that Nancy knew it was George's ringmaster whistle!

"Sorry," Alberto said as he handed the whistle to George.

Suddenly a frantic Peggy Bingle walked by.

"This is terrible!" Peggy was telling herself. "Simply terrible!"

"What's terrible, Ms. Bingle?" Nancy asked.

Peggy stopped and said, "The Fabuloso twins sprinkled itching powder in Ringmaster Rex's suit. He's refusing to do the show today!"

"Oh no!" Alberto said. "Who will blow the whistle to start the circus?"

George flashed a grin, and then she stuck the

shiny silver ringmaster whistle in her mouth. She puffed her cheeks and—

TWEEEEEEEEEEEEEEEEEEEEEEEEEEE!

"Oh my!" Peggy said, clapping both hands over her ears. Nancy and Bess smiled as they covered their ears too.

"Does that answer your question, Ms. Bingle?" George asked with a grin.

More circus people came out of their trailers to see what the noise was all about. Ringmaster Rex ran over too, itching and scratching all the way.

"Well, now," Rex told George, "I see you found your missing whistle."

"It's the real deal, Ringmaster Rex," Nancy said. "Now maybe you can give George another chance at being junior ringmaster."

"I can do better than that," Rex said with a grin. "George can be the *only* ringmaster in the show today!"

"Serious?" George gasped.

"Serious!" Rex replied. "Or . . . at least until I get a new suit."

"I have an idea too," Alberto said as he turned to Nancy and Bess. "How would you two like to be in the Oodles of Poodles act today?"

"Us?" Bess gasped.

"What would we do?" Nancy asked excitedly.

"You can hold the hoop while the dogs jump through," Alberto explained.

"Fun!" Bess cried happily.

"Oodles of fun!" Nancy exclaimed.

"Your ringmaster suit is still in your trailer, George," Peggy said. "I'll knock on your door when it's show time."

"Thanks, Ms. Bingle!" George said. "I know the drill!"

The circus people left to get ready for the show, and Nancy, Bess, and George high-fived. The Clue Crew had solved another case, but that wasn't all. . . .

"We're all going to be in the circus!" Nancy cheered. "How superamazingly cool is that?"

"I wonder what we're going to wear," Bess said excitedly.

"From now on I'm wearing my whistle around my neck!" George said. "After all, a good ring-master never goes anywhere without her whistle."

"And a good detective," Nancy said with a smile, "never goes anywhere without her Clue Book!"